SMALL TOWN JUSTICE

VALERIE HANSEN

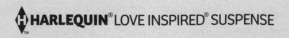

™ LOVE INSPIRED BOOKS

Recycling programs for this product may not exist in your area.

ISBN-13: 978-0-373-44714-5

Small Town Justice

Copyright © 2016 by Valerie Whisenand

This edition published by arrangement with Love Inspired Books.

® and TM are trademarks of Love Inspired Books, used under license. Trademarks indicated with ® are registered in the United States Patent and Trademark Office, the Canadian Intellectual Property Office and in other countries.

www.Harlequin.com

Printed in U.S.A.

Ask and God will give you.
Search, and you will find.
Knock and the door will open for you.
—Matthew 7:7

To my Joe, who is with me in spirit, looking over my shoulder and offering moral support as I write. He always will be.

And thanks to my dear friend Karen for keeping me on the right track—as much as possible!

ONE

The narrow dirt track leading to the deserted farm was so overgrown, so cloaked in shadows, Jamie Lynn almost missed her turn. Seeing the decrepit condition of the well-loved house broke her heart.

Parking her mini pickup, she shivered and stared. Well, what had she expected? Nobody had lived there for almost fifteen years. Not since her family had been split apart by lies and she'd been sent to live with an elderly aunt.

The little white dog beside her whimpered.

Jamie Lynn instinctively stroked his head. "Yes, this is it, Ulysses."

He began to pant and wiggle all over. "Okay, you can come with me while I have a look around," she told him, slipping her cell phone into her jeans pocket. "Hold still so I can get your harness unclipped."

He continued to strain and squirm. "I'm about to give up and leave you," she warned. "Sit. Stay."

He sat. He did not stay long. The moment she shifted her attention to the leash lying on the floor of the pickup's cab, he leaped over her, using her back as a springboard, and landed on the hard-packed ground like a gymnast making a competition dismount.

"Ulysses! No!"

Jamie Lynn chased him through the tall grass and weeds, ruing the fact that her clothing was summer-light shorts, a T-top and sandals.

"Ulysses," she wheedled, trying to sound unperturbed. "Come on, baby. I'm not mad. I just don't want to lose you."

Ahead, she heard him yip. "Please, *please* don't catch anything bigger than you are."

She rounded the house. The roof over the back porch had partially collapsed but she spotted a flash of white fur as her dog ducked through the half-open door.

Normally, Jamie wouldn't have considered entering someone else's house without an invitation. However, since her research had shown that this place had long ago been seized for unpaid taxes and didn't belong to any individual, she figured it would be okay to venture inside long enough to catch her naughty dog.

The staccato cadence of his nails led her to the stairway, where his paws had left impressions in the dust. Jamie followed. Pausing at the top of the stairs, she was overcome with nostalgia for her childhood home.

"Marf!"

Ulysses's sharp, single bark snapped her back to the present and drew her to her former bedroom. He was circling excitedly in front of one of the tall, narrow windows as if insisting she must look.

Below, parking behind her pickup, was a larger truck with a camouflage paint job. Two men climbed out.

They were both carrying rifles. *Uh-oh.*

Jamie's heart began to pound. She tried to lift the warped wooden sash and was barely able to move it.

Before she had a chance to shout hello through the

narrow opening, let alone begin an apology, she overheard one of the men speaking. His gruff words made the hair on the nape of her neck prickle.

"That's her license number. We know she got here."

"Yeah? So where'd she disappear to?"

The first man cursed. "Probably the house. Let's go."

"I don't like it. Suppose somebody sees us hanging around and makes a connection later?"

"If things turn ugly we'll ditch her truck. Nobody will suspect she ever made it this far."

Jamie Lynn was afraid to breathe. These men had known she was coming to Serenity. Who, of the few people she'd contacted to ask about her family history, would send thugs after her? And *why*?

Easing aside so she wouldn't be spotted from below, Jamie watched one of the men making a cell phone call. While he talked, the other began stabbing at her truck's tires. Then they started for the house and disappeared beneath the overhang of the porch roof.

She heard wood splintering. The stomping of heavy hiking boots. They'd smashed the front door. They were coming for her!

It took only seconds to dial 911 and rasp in the address and that she was in trouble. But she knew there was no chance anyone from town could reach her in time to intervene. Not unless she hid long enough for help to arrive. *But where?*

Voices from downstairs sent rumbling echoes throughout the empty structure. Cracking, banging, background noises indicated that the men planned to take the old house apart, piece by piece, until they found her.

What could she possibly do?

Memories of growing up in the old house carried Jamie Lynn back to childhood and the simple games of hide-and-go-seek she and her big brother had played. *The downstairs maid's closet!* Their favorite hiding place was perfectly camouflaged. Only how was she going to reach it without being seen?

So terrified she could hardly draw a usable breath, she tiptoed down the hall to the antiquated bathroom, eased the door shut behind her, then whispered to her nervous dog and held him close. "Easy, boy. Shush."

All she could do was wait.

Aunt Tessie would have urged her to pray, she knew, yet no inspiring spiritual words came to mind. Jamie Lynn wasn't surprised. God had quit heeding her prayers when she was ten years old.

If He had been listening to her back then, she knew she wouldn't have lost her whole family.

Shane Colton parked his flatbed tow truck beyond the small pickup with four flat tires and hit the ground running, waving his arms to get the sheriff's attention. "Harlan! I just saw two men in hunter's camo run out the back."

"Must've spotted us," Sheriff Allgood replied. "Let 'em go. We've got their truck for ID."

"I didn't recognize either one." Glancing at the old house, Shane frowned. "Aren't you going in?"

"In a minute. Gotta radio the station so my officers know to keep their eyes peeled for two guys on foot."

Uneasy, Shane lifted his chin. Sniffed the breeze. And instantly knew what was happening. *Smoke!*

Hands cupped around his mouth, he shouted, "Call the fire department," as he raced toward the house.

"Stop! Don't!"

He ignored the sheriff's command. If he hurried, he might be able to put the fire out while it was small. If not, he could at least do a quick search of the premises for victims. Somebody had made the report of trouble at the old Henderson farm. That person might still be inside.

What was wrong with Ulysses all of a sudden? "Take it easy, boy. We're safe now. I heard them leave."

The lapdog's tiny claws raked Jamie Lynn's forearm. "Ouch! Knock it off," she snapped, immediately penitent. He'd kept quiet while she'd tiptoed down the stairs and hidden them both in the maid's cupboard. It was time to let him be himself again.

"Okay, okay." She got to her knees and operated the panel that masked the secret opening. It slid back silently, revealing disaster. The walls and ceilings were partially obscured by layers of drifting smoke. They had to get out of there.

Startled, Ulysses twisted from her grasp and disappeared into the smoke, barking.

"No!"

She started to rise from her crawl on the floor. Thicker, acrid vapor made her gag and drop back down. Tears blinded her further. There was no way she'd be able to spot her little dog in that swirling, glowing haze. If he didn't come back to her, the poor baby was going to die! And it was her fault.

Rasping, gagging, Jamie did her best to scream, "Ulysses?" He didn't respond. Was it already too late?

Brokenhearted, she started to inch farther into the

thick of things, moving by feel and hoping that her next reach might be long enough to touch his soft fur.

She could not give up. Not as long as there was one more breath left to keep her moving. Coughs racked her body, aching all the way to her ribs and beyond. Thoughts of her parents and brother, R.J., swirled in her mind, and confusion surrounded her, beginning to deaden the pain.

Then, suddenly, she was grasped around the waist and jerked sideways.

Fighting spirit returned. Jamie kicked and struck out at her captor. She even managed a feeble screech.

Spots of bright light flickered in her distorted vision and she felt as if she were floating. Cradled in powerful arms, she heard the strong beating of a heart.

Brightness abruptly bathed her face and she wondered if this was the phenomenon often reported by those having near-death experiences.

Surrendering, she laid her head against the shoulder of her captor and slipped into unconsciousness.

It had been several years since Shane Colton had practiced CPR but everything came back to him in a rush. He laid the woman on the ground, tilted her head to make sure her airway was clear, then pressed his lips to hers and delivered several rescue breaths before checking her pulse.

"Ambulance is almost here," Harlan shouted. "Is she alive?"

To Shane's immense relief he was able to reply, "Yes!"

"I oughta slap the cuffs on you for pullin' a stunt like that," the sheriff said. "What would your little boy do if his daddy went and got himself killed? Huh? You ever think of that?"

Shane shook his head. Harlan was absolutely right. A single parent needed to be extra careful. He would never purposely endanger Kyle's future. The poor little guy had been too small to miss his mother much after she'd left them, but losing his only remaining parent would be devastating, even though he'd still have loving grandparents.

"I wasn't thinking. I just did what I thought was necessary," Shane said.

"How'd you find the victim in all that smoke?"

"Heard a dog barking," Shane told him. "You got any water in your car?"

Harlan handed him a small bottle and stood back while Shane trickled some onto the woman's face and gently wiped it with a clean bandanna.

Off to his right, trying to bark and mostly squeaking instead, was a sooty, dusty mongrel. "You may be a sorry excuse for a dog, little guy, but you did your part today."

Still kneeling beside her, Shane gazed at the young woman. Even with reddened cheeks and soot and water streaking her face, it was clear that she was a beauty. He'd never seen hair that silky or quite that dark.

So who was she and what had she been doing inside the abandoned house? He frowned. A better question might be, what did those creeps in camo have against her?

Sirens heralded the arrival of the sheriff's backup units and the ambulance so Shane reluctantly relinquished his place to the team of paramedics and stood aside. As soon as they had checked the victim's vital signs, they put her on a gurney, began administering oxygen and pushed her toward the waiting ambulance.

"Is she going to be okay?" Shane asked, following.

One of the medics nodded. "She's trying to talk. That's a good sign. Keeps saying she's worried about a white dog."

"I can get him. Are you transporting to Fulton County Hospital?"

"Yeah. They'll send her on if necessary."

Shane approached the mini pickup and noticed the excited dog racing toward him. He opened the driver's-side door and stood back. The dog leaped in. What a relief. Of all the things he'd tried to do that day, catching a half-wild pup had turned out to be the easiest.

Fire trucks were arriving. He hailed Harlan. "The dog's out of the way. Want me to go ahead and haul her truck back to my place?"

"Yeah. Lock it in your service yard, then come back for this other one. I'll stop and check them after I'm done here."

"Gotcha. I thought I'd drop her dog by the vet's and make sure it's okay, too."

"You're the one with the kid at home. You should keep him."

"No, thanks." Shane was smiling more broadly. "Did you happen to hear what she called it when she was talking to the medics?"

Harlan chuckled. "Sounded like Useless to me. That name sure fits."

Shane totally agreed.

Jamie Lynn had fought her way out of the fog clouding her brain. By the time she was delivered to the emergency room, her eyes had been bathed to soothe them and she was able to sit up on her own.

"I told you, I'm fine," she insisted between bouts of coughing that doubled her over.

"I'll be checking you out to be sure," an amiable nurse said. "Can you tell me your name?"

"Jamie Lynn Nolan. I have my ID in my purse. It's in my truck."

"Do you remember what happened?"

Jamie touched her forehead. It felt gritty. "Yes. Two men were after me. I hid and they set the house on fire."

"That's pretty much the story I got from the sheriff," the nurse told her. "I'll ask him to bring your things to you here. How's that?"

"Wait!" Jamie grabbed her forearm. "They have to find my little dog." Tears began to fill her eyes and trickle down her cheeks. "Ulysses was with me inside the house and I don't know…" More coughing interrupted her as she buried her face in her hands.

The nurse gently patted her shoulder. "Okay. Wait right here. I'll go find out what I can."

The weight of her anticipated loss was so burdensome, Jamie Lynn wondered how she could bear it. *Poor little Ulysses.* She drew up her legs, clasped them in front of her and rested her forehead on her skinned knees. Aunt Tessie had warned her against stirring up the past, but she hadn't listened. And now her stubbornness and curiosity had cost her the life of her very best friend.

More bits of fractured memory began to drift into place and fit together. She recalled being lifted and carried from the burning house. At the time she'd tried to resist, but whoever had rescued her had continued to treat her gently. He had delivered his own air to her burning lungs and forced her to breathe again. Whoever it had been deserved her lifelong gratitude.

Jamie didn't know how long she'd sat there, lost in thought. It must have been a long time because when her nurse reappeared she was carrying the purse from the truck.

"You found my things!"

"Sure did. *All* of them."

As the nurse stepped aside another figure came into view; a well-built man about six feet tall. He seemed familiar. Had she looked into those warm brown eyes before?

"This is my friend Shane," the nurse told Jamie. "He's the guy who saved you."

New moisture bathed Jamie's reddened, smarting eyes. She didn't try to hide it. This man was her hero and she wanted him to know how grateful she was.

As he stepped closer, she reached out. He clasped her hand, their gazes locking, their connection evident.

"I don't know how to thank you," she whispered hoarsely.

"No thanks necessary. I'm just glad the good Lord led me to be there when I was needed."

"I wish my little dog had been rescued, too."

The grin that instantly illuminated his handsome face gave her new hope. Her eyes widened. Her grip on his hand tightened. "You *found* him?"

Shane nodded. "Yes.

"He's okay? I mean, he wasn't burned?"

"That long hair got singed and he was more gray than white, but the vet says that's basically all. They'll take care of him until you can pick him up."

Elated beyond her most fantastic dreams, Jamie Lynn

swung her feet off the side of the exam table, threw her arms around her rescuer and hugged him as tightly as she could. Several seconds passed before she felt the answering pressure of his broad hand patting her back.

"Thank you, thank you, thank you!" She leaned away to look into his eyes again. "I don't know how I can ever pay you back, but I promise to try."

He eased away and looked as if he might be blushing.

"I meant, maybe I can treat you to a nice dinner out once they spring me from this place," she explained. "And your family, of course. The more the merrier."

"It's just me and my son, Kyle," Shane said. "We'd love to go out to eat with you. If you're well enough, how about this Sunday after church?"

"Well, I… I mean I don't usually go to church. I used to when I was little but…"

He raked his fingers through his wavy, light brown hair. "No sweat. Sorry if I made you uncomfortable."

Jamie was about to reply when he handed her a business card.

"I have your truck. Take this so you'll know how to reach me when you're ready. Are you planning to be in Serenity long?"

"I'm not sure," she said, continuing to smile. "I've rented a room at the motel."

"Great. When the doctors release you, the sheriff or I can give you a lift. He'll need to take your statement, too."

"I can't imagine what I might be able to tell him that he doesn't already know." She sobered. "Has he tracked down the arsonists yet?"

"I don't think so. But he will. We both grew up here, so we know everybody in Serenity."

It was then that Jamie Lynn glanced down at the card he'd given her. His last name was *Colton*?

She repeated it aloud. "Colton? Any relation to the man who used to be sheriff?" she asked, wondering if her voice would have sounded so shaky without the throat irritation.

"Yeah. Sam was my dad. He was quite a guy."

He sure was, Jamie thought, clenching her jaw and wondering what strange quirk of nature had put her in such an untenable position.

She now owed her very life to a man whose family had destroyed hers, one lie at a time.

TWO

Shane brought his personal pickup to a stop under the hospital's front portico and let it idle while he stepped inside. As Harlan had promised, the woman he'd rescued the day before was waiting. When she glanced up and saw him, she was clearly surprised. And not terribly pleased.

"I thought the sheriff was coming to pick me up."

"He was." Puzzled, Shane ventured a smile. "He got another call and asked me to stand in for him. I'm a volunteer. Hope that's okay."

"Oh." She got to her feet, shouldered her purse and reached for a small plastic bag.

"Let me get that for you."

"I can handle it. It's just laundry." Although her words sounded brusque, she did add, "Thanks."

"So that's why you're dressed in scrubs."

"Yes."

Shane lost his chance to hold the lobby door for her because it was automated, so he hurried to his pickup to open the passenger side.

As soon as she was settled, he smiled again. "I thought we'd stop at the vet and get Useless before I took you to your motel."

Her eyes narrowed. "What did you call him?"

"Useless. That's his name, isn't it?" He chuckled briefly. "I must say, it fits."

"His name is *Ulysses*," Jamie Lynn told him flatly.

That sounded so funny in contrast to what he'd been told, he laughed again. "If you say so, ma'am."

"I certainly do."

"Okeydokey. Do you need help with your seat belt?"

"No, I can manage." She turned aside to cough, and Shane was sorry to hear the raspy breathing that accompanied it.

"How are you feeling?"

"A lot better than I sound. Thanks for asking. I'm supposed to follow up with my family doctor in a few days."

"Will you be leaving, then?"

"No. If I don't stop wheezing soon I'll find a local practitioner." She sighed audibly, triggering another bout of coughing.

"We're not short on doctors around here," Shane told her. "Pharmacies, either. Didn't they prescribe anything for you?"

"Just over-the-counter syrups. I'll be fine once I get Ulysses back and you've repaired my tires."

"They'll all need to be replaced," Shane stated flatly. "Did you look at what was done to them?"

"I saw a man stabbing them with a knife. I was too far away to tell how badly they were damaged."

"Let's just say they wouldn't even make a good planter in a hillbilly's front yard."

"That bad, huh?"

"Actually, worse." Shane could tell she was worried.

"I've got a buddy in the tire business. Want me to ask him if he has a new or used set that will fit your truck?"

"As long as you two don't try to sell me oceanfront property in Arizona or something like that."

Shane held up a hand as if taking an oath. "No tricks. I promise. This is a small town. Our reputations are very important." He began to grin. "Besides, we all trust each other around here."

"Is that why you left this pickup running in front of the hospital? If you tried that most places it wouldn't be there when you came out."

"Serenity isn't most places."

To his surprise, his passenger averted her face and muttered, "You can say *that* again."

Jamie Lynn's reunion with her dog was tearful yet joyful. When neither the veterinarian nor the groomer who had washed him would accept payment she was astonished.

"Told you so," Shane said on their way out.

She buried her face in Ulysses's soft, clean fur. "I don't get it. Those people don't know me. Why should they waive their normal fees?"

"Maybe because I explained the situation when I left Useless with them."

"You're determined to call him that, aren't you?"

Looking at his profile, she could see half of a wide grin. "Yup. I like to see steam shoot out of your ears."

"Fine. Suit yourself. I don't imagine you and I will have much reason to talk again after you've fixed my truck, anyway."

"Oh, I don't know." He shrugged. "It's a pretty small

town. If you hang around, we're bound to run into each other."

What Jamie wanted to say was, *Not if I can help it*, but she kept that thought to herself. It seemed impossible that a man as astute as Shane Colton had not yet put together enough clues to guess her former identity. Or had he? she wondered. It was remotely possible that he'd figured out her lineage and was toying with her. Was he the kind of man who would be purposely devious?

She honestly didn't think so, not that she considered herself the best judge of truthfulness. After all, Aunt Tessie had lied to her for years about what had become of her parents and she'd believed every word.

Clutching Ulysses, she murmured endearments and let him lick her under the chin. He was clearly so glad they were reunited he could hardly sit still. Jamie Lynn sympathized. She was feeling such a strong sense of unrest she wanted to fling open the door and escape from the moving vehicle. The mere thought of such drastic action was unnerving. What was wrong with her? Shane, the hospital staff, the sheriff, the vet—everybody in Serenity had been so nice.

Yeah, if you didn't count the men who had said they were going to get rid of her, one way or another.

"Speaking of small towns, what's the latest on the two guys who set the fire?" she asked.

"Their truck was a dead end. It had been stolen that morning." He glanced across at her. "What were you doing wandering around out there in the first place?"

"Like I told the sheriff, I was exploring and thought the abandoned house looked interesting."

"Uh-huh."

"You don't sound convinced." And neither had Harlan Allgood when he'd questioned her, but at least he hadn't pressed for details that might have revealed her past before she was ready to do so.

"I might buy that if nothing bad had happened to you while you were poking around."

"Guess I was in the wrong place at the wrong time." The whole truth would become obvious to everyone soon enough and she didn't want to distract him while he was driving. Besides, she felt safer in Shane's company and wanted to stay on his good side, not that that made much sense.

"That would do it," Jamie muttered, realizing belatedly that she had actually voiced her conclusion.

One quick peek told her he had heard. Before he could start asking more questions, she said, "In case I didn't tell you yesterday, thanks for saving my neck."

"I got the idea you were grateful," he replied.

A flush of color on his cheeks reminded her of the way she'd thrown herself into his arms after hearing that her little dog was safe and well.

"That hug was for saving Ulysses," Jamie insisted, once again burying her face in the small dog's silky fur.

"If you say so."

"I do. He's family." The moment those words were out, she realized she'd opened another can of worms.

"What about the people in your life?" Shane asked.

"I—uh—I was raised by my great-aunt."

"Your parents…?"

"Are gone," she said, using the familiar expression to tell the truth while giving the impression both were deceased. For all she knew they might be.

"I'm sorry."

Jamie Lynn nodded. "Me, too. So, how far is it to my truck? And how long will it take you to fix it?"

"I thought you'd want to go back to the motel. You know, kick back and rest. Maybe grab some lunch."

"I ate at the hospital and I've done nothing but rest since yesterday. What I need is wheels."

"Fine. We'll swing by the garage I own so you can see the tire damage for yourself. Believe me, I'm not exaggerating. Nobody could repair those cuts."

"Do you accept credit cards?"

"Sure. We may be rural but we aren't primitive."

Jamie couldn't help smiling. "Oh? You could have fooled me." They were passing the antebellum courthouse and modest businesses around the old square. "This place looks like it belongs in history books."

"It does. One of the battles of the Civil War was fought on Pilot Hill." He leaned over the steering wheel and pointed. "Right up there where the radio towers are now. See the flashing beacons?"

"Yes." Leaning back against the seat, she closed her eyes and sighed. There was another page of Serenity's history that interested her far more—the one that involved her brother and both parents.

As soon as news got out that she was in town to investigate the crime that had destroyed her family, chances were that most folks wouldn't want to talk to her, let alone offer their help. The current sheriff had studied her as if he were close to figuring out who she really was when he'd interviewed her in the hospital. It was only a matter of time until somebody remembered Jamie Lynn *Henderson*, put two and two together and got four.

Correction, Jamie Lynn thought. Someone had already added it up. Whether her attackers had found her at the old farm or followed her there, their orders had been clear. They'd said it themselves. It was their job to eliminate her before she made any progress on her brother R.J.'s behalf.

Progress that might not only prove her big brother was innocent of vehicular homicide but also point the finger of guilt at someone else.

She knew she was on the right track precisely *because* they had sent thugs after her. Although her enemies might be ruthless, they were functioning on an emotional level rather than a rational one. As long as she kept her wits about her and stayed out of abandoned buildings, chances were she'd eventually dredge up enough truth to help her brother get a new trial. In a new venue.

She glanced at her handsome companion, chagrined that her goal was to disprove the accepted story of his father's death. But could she trust him?

Who she could and couldn't trust in that town was one of the *first* things she needed to know. Confiding in the wrong person could be worse than doing nothing.

As the hours passed, Shane was beginning to think the young woman was never going to ask to be taken to her motel. Considering the way she'd made herself and Useless comfortable in his tiny waiting room, he wondered if she intended to spend the entire afternoon. That would have been troubling by itself. Added to the concentrated attention she was giving him and his workers, it was getting downright creepy.

He pulled out his cell phone and punched in the number of his buddy Charlie.

"Tire shop."

"It's Shane again. Any word on those tires I called about?"

"You asked me the same thing an hour ago," Charlie said. "Keep your shirt on. I've checked my own inventory and don't have four alike but I think I've located a good used set in Batesville."

"Think, or know?" Shane eyed his office through the grimy window between it and the garage. Being the only auto repair shop in town sometimes had its drawbacks. "It looks like she is planning to sit right here until I get her truck back on the road."

"So?"

"So, I don't like it."

"What's the matter, is she ugly?"

Shane shook his head and turned his back on the window. "No. She's actually a knockout."

"So, she's raising a ruckus?"

"Not that, either. There's just something strange about her. Maybe it's the way she's been staring at me. I don't know."

"You saved her life, right?"

Shane nodded. "Yeah."

"Then I wouldn't worry. She's probably got a bad case of hero worship."

"I suppose that could be it." He raked his fingers through his hair. "Give me a call as soon as you know anything definite, will you?"

"If she's as pretty as you say, why not just enjoy her company?" He chuckled. "If I wasn't so busy here I'd drop by and take her off your hands."

Shane was shaking his head as he said, "No way. She's not that kind of woman. She's… I don't know, sort of fragile."

"Skinny?"

"Not at all. I can't explain it. All I know is she seems lost. Even lonely. The first time she opened her eyes and looked up at me after the fire she reminded me of an injured deer surrounded by a pack of hungry coyotes."

"Sounds to me like you're as scrambled as she is. I'll get back to you ASAP."

"Okay. Thanks." Shane pivoted when he heard the back door slam.

A bundle of energy raced toward him, arms raised, and Shane swung his five-year-old son off the ground. "Hey, buddy. Why are you here so early?"

"Memaw's gonna go get beautiful."

"Did you tell her she already is?"

Kyle's head bobbed, making his honey-blond curls bounce. "Uh-huh. But she didn't believe me."

Holding the boy close, Shane looked past him to smile at Marsha. "Hey, Mom, we both think you're pretty enough."

"Well, I don't. Look at all the gray in my hair. I don't want Otis to start thinking he married an old lady." She began to fan her overly rosy cheeks and giggle like a love-struck teenager.

It had pleased Shane when his widowed mother had finally fallen in love again and remarried, but it was still hard to picture Otis Bryce as a father figure, let alone see his own mother as a blushing bride. Just short of turning thirty, he'd pictured people his mother's age as too old to care about romance.

About to reassure her about her good looks, Shane was stopped by a shrill squeal next to his ear.

"A puppy!" Kyle was squirming in his arms and pointing at the waiting room. "Let me go see!"

It took Shane a second to realize why the boy was so excited. "That dog belongs to the lady who's holding him."

"Okay." He continued to struggle against Shane's restraint. "I wanna pet him. Can I, Daddy? Can I? Please…?"

Taking the child's hand, he cautioned him, "All right. Just go slowly and don't yell or you might scare him."

"Puppies love kids. Everybody says."

"Well, that dog isn't a pup. He's all grown up. And sometimes little dogs bite because they get scared. We need to ask the lady if you can pet him and do whatever she says. Understand?"

"Uh-huh."

The five-year-old was leaning forward, dragging his reluctant father along as if he were towing a semi-truck behind a tricycle. Shane saw his customer gather up her pet and stand. Although she had looked wary when Kyle had screeched, she was currently smiling.

"This must be your son," Jamie Lynn said.

The child beamed. "I'm Kyle. I wanna play with your dog!"

"Can you play nicely and be careful you don't hurt him? He's getting kind of old."

"Daddy told me."

"Kyle thinks every small dog is a puppy," Shane explained. "I told him that Useless was all grown up."

She cradled her beloved fur ball as she sat again, placing the wiggly white mound on her lap. "Let him smell your hand before you try to touch him so he knows you're friendly."

Ulysses sniffed, then started to lick the boy all the way from his fingertips to his wrist.

Kyle broke into gales of laughter. "It tickles."

"What did you have for lunch?" Jamie Lynn asked.

"Um, a burger and a corn dog."

"Both? What about vegetables or fruit?"

"I hate bedj-tables. Yuck."

Shane could tell his customer wasn't pleased with his son's apparently haphazard diet. He knew he didn't need to make excuses to a stranger, yet for some reason he wanted her approval.

"We were in a hurry this morning, partly because I still had a man out sick and was handling the tow truck again, so I fed him a corn dog," Shane said. "I assume the burger was part of his school lunch."

"Uh-uh," the boy said. "Memaw bought it for me when she picked me up."

Marsha piped up. "I have a hair appointment." She patted her short locks and began to grin at the other woman. "You don't approve of fast food?"

"Sorry. I have a degree in early childhood development and sometimes advice just slips out. Proper nutrition is critical, especially in the formative years."

Shane had heard enough. "Look. I'm a single parent and I'm doing the best I can, okay? He's happy and healthy."

"It's actually more than that," Jamie Lynn said.

He watched her eyes begin to glisten. She had to be one of the most changeable women he'd ever met—more unpredictable than Ozark weather.

Just as he was preparing to defend himself further,

she sighed and added, "I can see that you've given him something else that many children lack."

"And what would that be?"

"Love," she told him, speaking softly. "All the vitamins in the world can't take the place of that."

THREE

The rush of emotions the little boy had triggered had almost destroyed Jamie Lynn's self-control. When he'd wrapped his arms around her neck to thank her for letting him pet her dog, she'd had to fight to keep from weeping for the loving family she'd lost so long ago.

It was this *town*, she reasoned. That was what was bothering her. She'd not only cheated death since arriving in Serenity, she'd done it in the very place where she'd spent her childhood. Of course she'd be upset. Confused. Perhaps a tad emotionally unstable. There was nothing disturbing about that. Instead of wasting energy dwelling on what she'd lost, she should be trying to figure out who wanted to get rid of her. Given the seriousness of that, all her other worries paled.

"I guess I'll give up and head over to the motel," she announced to Shane after he had settled his son in his private office with crayons and a coloring book.

She glanced at her truck, still sitting on flattened tires. "I don't imagine you'll be able to get me back on the road today."

"Nope."

"How far is it to the motel?"

His noncommittal shrug gave her the notion that she may have used up her chances to hitch a ride. "I can walk. Just point me in the right direction."

Shane sighed. "I'll take you. But right now I have to finish this job and line up tomorrow's schedule." He glanced at his watch. "Give me forty-five minutes."

"It's okay. Really it is. I walk all the time to exercise Ulysses."

The stern look he gave her was unexpected. "Look, lady, you spent the night in the hospital after somebody disabled your truck and tried to barbecue you. Since Harlan has no idea who's to blame, don't you think it would be wise to keep a low profile?"

Jamie Lynn tried to mask the shiver that shot through her by gathering up her purse. "I thought the sheriff was convinced those guys were just local boys acting reckless. That's the impression he gave me."

"He may be convinced, but I'm not," Shane said quietly. "Now sit down and wait for me the way I waited for you all afternoon."

An urge to snap to attention, salute and shout, "Yes, sir," came over her. With effort, Jamie was able to nod and appear compliant. She hated taking orders, particularly from folks she hardly knew, and her offbeat wit was overly fond of lightening that burden with problematic humor.

This time, however, she held it in check. Shane Colton had been nothing but nice to her and the more she let him do on her behalf, the more guilt piled up on her side of the equation. He was bound to be livid by the time he learned she was R.J.'s sister.

Nevertheless, she reasoned, limited options were keeping them together. If there had been anywhere else nearby to have her truck repaired, she'd have gotten away from him immediately. Even the tire store was thirty miles south. It made no sense to have her vehicle taken there when it was already in good hands.

Shane's hands *were* good, she affirmed without hesitation. Judging by all the business he had coming and going, his reputation was sterling.

A perverse part of her wished he were not quite so honest or approachable or considerate. It would be a lot easier to work against the prejudices of this town if she didn't have to worry about hurting such an amenable man.

Remember what the people here did to you and your poor family, she reminded herself. *They banded together to convict your brother—and Shane Colton is one of them.*

Jamie Lynn raised her eyes to watch him working. As little as twenty-four hours ago she'd had no trouble classifying Shane as just another narrow-minded local. Somehow, in that short span of time, she had begun seeing him as almost a friend, almost a potential ally. That was ridiculous, of course.

Trembling, yet decisive, Jamie Lynn snapped the leash on Ulysses before picking him up, got to her feet, smoothed the hem of the hospital garb she'd borrowed and walked straight out the door of the waiting room.

It was time to come clean.

Shane was startled when he heard someone at his elbow say, "Excuse me?"

"I told you I had a few things to see to before we left. Be patient, okay?"

"It's not that," she said. "I need to talk to you. Privately."

Something in her tone slipped through his concentration and pulled him from his work as effectively as a lasso tightening around the neck of a bucking bronco. His glance swept the work area then returned to her. "This is about as private as it gets. What's wrong?"

"I don't want you to think I've been deceiving you."

"Don't tell me your truck is stolen."

"No, no. Nothing like that." She'd tucked Ulysses under her arm and was petting him.

"Won't this wait?"

"Not really."

"We can talk later while I drive you home."

He saw her shake her head and marveled at the way her dark hair caught the light and gleamed as it moved. It was evident that once this woman got a notion to do or say something, nothing could stop her. "Okay. I'm listening."

"My name used to be Jamie Lynn *Henderson* instead of Nolan."

Scowling, Shane stared at her. "Okay."

"I don't think you fully understand," she said.

Shane sensed the crackle of tension in the air and noted her easing away from him, although she'd barely moved. He faced her and folded his arms across his chest. "Spell it out for me."

"*Henderson* doesn't ring a bell?"

"There's a town near Lake Norfork by that name."

"Think closer to home, Shane. My mother's name is Alice. Ray is my dad. And my brother is Ray Junior."

Sensing that he was gaping at her, he snapped his jaw closed. "You're *that* Henderson?"

"Yes."

"Hold on. I don't remember any daughter named Jamie Lynn."

"Probably because my family always called me Baby Sister. I was in kindergarten before I knew that wasn't my given name."

"Why the charade?" Anger was building. Shane fought to keep it from spilling over and halting their conversation before he could learn more.

"It wasn't a trick," Jamie vowed. "My great-aunt adopted me years ago and gave me her last name. That's why I can't figure out why I was targeted so quickly after I hit town. It must be because I called the courthouse to inquire about my family and ask for the transcripts of my brother's trial."

"Go on." His arms remained crossed, his eyes narrowing.

"I was kept in the dark as a child. When I was recently told that my mother ran away to save herself after my father disappeared, right here in your precious town, I decided to come back and see what else I could find out."

"That's crazy talk."

"Is it? What if my brother wasn't driving the car that hit your dad?"

"Don't be ridiculous. He was not only tried and convicted, he confessed."

"Because he was threatened. So were my parents. Mom sent me to live with an aunt in New England during the trial to keep me out of danger."

"That doesn't prove a thing except that your mom was paranoid. Maybe your whole family was."

As he continued to observe her, he saw her scan the

parts of the garage she could see from where they stood. She was plainly nervous. Wary. Uncomfortable. Considering what she'd just admitted, he didn't blame her.

If he'd had the option he would gladly have hauled her truck to another garage and washed his hands of her.

It didn't dawn on him that his thoughts were so transparent until she said, "Look. I know you don't really want to deal with my problems anymore. Try to think of me as just another nameless customer. Once we get through this, I promise I won't bother you again."

"Of course you will."

"I don't understand."

A deep breath and heavy sigh helped settle him enough to speak his mind without letting rancor overwhelm him. "You don't have to tell me more about why you came back. You intend to stir up trouble. It's a given, particularly now that I've seen how you operate."

"Oh, really?"

"Yes. Really. Once you latch on to an idea, you haven't got sense enough to drop it, even when it's wrong."

"Listen, Mr. Colton. The folks around here were so sure R.J. was guilty they did that very thing to him. He was convicted in the court of public opinion long before he ever stood before a judge."

"Not true. He had a fair trial. I was there."

Her shoulders slumped, and she looked away as if viewing the past before she said, "Sadly, I was not. My parents thought they were sparing me by keeping me in the dark. All they were really doing was giving my imagination free rein. That was a mistake. Now I have to go back and start from the beginning if I want to understand."

"How do you propose to do that?"

"Court records, among other things. As I said, I've already talked to people at the county courthouse and requested other information that's in the public domain."

"Terrific." He knew he was scowling and gave himself permission to continue. "My mother is just getting her life back together and you come along to ruin it."

"This has nothing to do with your mother."

His voice rose. "She was married to the man your brother ran down and left in the street to bleed to death. How can you say it has nothing to do with her? It has *everything* to do with her."

Serenity had two main streets and two highways that intersected. Jamie Lynn knew she was currently on Third Street and that her motel was located on Highway 62. As soon as Shane's back was turned, she slipped out the front door and headed toward courthouse square. From there, she figured she could easily get her bearings. There was no danger. Nobody would expect to see her dressed like a nurse just getting off duty.

One thing was definite. She was not going to spend one more unnecessary moment with any Colton if she could help it. This would mark a new beginning to her quest.

Ulysses trotted along beside her as if he'd strolled those roads all his life. As soon as they reached Church Street and could walk on sidewalks instead of the outside edges of narrow pavement, Jamie Lynn stopped worrying about passing traffic.

Looking down at her exuberant pet made her smile, as always. "What a good boy. I wish you could tell me how to relax the way you do," she crooned.

He rewarded her with a wag of his tail and a glance before continuing to sniff his way along their route.

The afternoon was still warm and the air so clean and fresh she could almost feel it healing her sore throat. There was also peace and ambience to be enjoyed here; something she had neither remembered nor expected.

Traffic circling the square was heavier than she had anticipated, so she paused. Proceeding directly to the courthouse would entail extra crossings. Sensibly, she opted to take the long way around instead.

Flashes of buried memory began to surface. A few stores and even nearby homes seemed familiar, and not in a negative way. The same thing had occurred when she'd been exploring the old farmhouse, but she had not expected to experience such clear recollections anywhere else.

"I'm supposed to hate this place," she muttered to herself, disgusted to be feeling almost comfortable.

A family was coming out of the tiny library, the excited children clasping books and dancing for joy. An older couple was entering the café on the west side of the square. The name over the restaurant door didn't ring a bell but the building itself certainly did.

Jamie looked ahead and saw a sign for the police station. *Good.* If she couldn't locate the motel once she turned the corner, she'd backtrack and ask someone in there for directions.

Cracks in the sidewalk where tree roots had lifted the paving slowed her briefly. That, and Ulysses's insistence that he sniff every post and corner and square inch of the walkway.

Steep concrete stairs led up to the glass doors of the police building. They, too, were familiar. Perhaps it would be prudent to check here before proceeding. After all, she was already on their doorstep.

Ulysses made the first couple of high jumps, then pulled back so she'd pick him up and carry him the rest of the way. Traffic continued to pass, the drivers cautious because there were no stop signs to regulate right of way on the corners.

Jamie got to the top landing. Tried the door. Found it locked.

With her dog still tucked under one arm, she used her opposite hand to shade her eyes and peer inside.

The building was vacant.

She put Ulysses down and began searching for an explanation. That was when she saw the crudely lettered, faded sign taped to one wall. The entire Serenity Police Department and the sheriff's office had moved to an address out of town on Highway 9!

From her higher vantage point she assessed her surroundings. Nine North bordered that side of the square. If she hadn't been on foot she'd have followed it then and there. However, as things stood, she supposed it would be best to keep going and locate her motel.

For the first time since abandoning Shane Colton she was starting to wish she'd let him drive her. The worst part of that notion was the realization she was behaving exactly the way he'd described. Foolish and stubborn.

Jamie Lynn murmured, "Oh, well, what's done is done," bending to scoop up her short-legged pet for the trip down the steep stairway.

A second before her hand touched him he yelped and jumped away.

Startled, Jamie was caught off balance. She lurched.

Dropped to her knees. Sensed an unmistakable ripple of fear. Was she simply reacting to the high-strung dog?

There was no time to speculate further.

Something crashed above her. Tiny shards of safety glass from the thick doors began to rain down.

She huddled over her little dog, unsure what had happened but taking her cues from him.

Together they crouched on the cement threshold, trembling, frightened, waiting.

Nothing more fell. Someone shouted from the street, "You all right, lady?"

She raised her head slightly to call, "I think so."

Bystanders were gathering on the sidewalk in front of the deserted building. Some were quiet. Others were talking or yelling.

A figure broke through their ranks and raced up the steps.

When Ulysses began to wiggle and wag his tail, Jamie made eye contact with the new arrival.

It was Shane Colton. And he looked mad enough to spit nails.

FOUR

Shane hovered over her. "You just had to do things your way again, didn't you?"

"Don't yell at me."

"Somebody ought to. What were you thinking? You couldn't be more vulnerable if you'd been carrying a sign that said Shoot Me."

"Ha-ha. Very funny."

"This is no joke." He offered his hand, wondering if she'd take it.

Jamie continued to crouch. "Is it safe now?"

"Yes. The shot came from a rusty blue pickup. It laid rubber all the way to the traffic light and kept going."

Her fingers closed around Shane's and he helped her rise. It wasn't too surprising to see her swaying as she regained her balance. He slipped an arm around her shoulders, telling himself it was merely to keep her from collapsing. "You okay?"

"Yes. I never dreamed anybody would recognize me dressed like this," she said, sounding breathless.

"It was probably easier because of Useless. I don't imagine there are many women with such dark hair and a dog that looks like a dust mop with legs. That's how I spotted you."

"You were following me?"

"I shouldn't have had to." He paused long enough to give her the once-over. "Are you sure you're not hurt?"

"My pride is pretty bruised," she said wryly.

"There's a lot of glass in your hair."

"Oh, dear."

When she started to reach up he stopped her by tenderly clasping her wrist. "You need to let the police see you just as you are. I'm sure somebody in the crowd has called them by now."

"Probably." Jamie Lynn sighed. "If they're not all too busy taking pictures with their phones."

Shane stepped in front of her, forming a human shield. "It's too late to keep your picture from ending up on the internet but we don't need to give your attackers any more reasons to gloat."

"Attackers? Plural again?"

He nodded soberly. "Looked like it. Judging by the direction the truck was heading, the driver couldn't have hit this door. It had to be a passenger who could lean out the window and aim higher."

"Wonderful. I suppose it's the same two guys who tried to toast me yesterday."

"There you go again," he said with a shake of his head. "Why are you making light of these attacks? Don't you realize that somebody is seriously trying to harm you?"

"Sure. Thing is, there's nothing I can do about it."

"Of course there is."

She ducked out from under his protective arm and faced him more fully. "If you mean I should run and hide the way my mother did, forget it. Not gonna happen."

"There's nothing cowardly about using your head

and being cautious. You act like you enjoy taunting whoever is out to hurt you."

Shane watched myriad emotions flit across her face, ending with stubbornness. "Look. Whether you believe it or not, my brother is innocent. This town conspired to ruin his life and destroy my family—and succeeded. After all that, I guess I've gotten fatalistic."

"What about trusting God? Maybe it was His plan to rescue you and you've interfered so much you're way off track."

The fire in her dark eyes and the set of her jaw told him plenty before she ever spoke.

"God gave up on me long ago."

"How can you say that?"

"Easy." Hearing the approach of sirens, Jamie Lynn scooped up Ulysses and started down the steep steps, one hand following the pipe railing for better balance. "I prayed for my big brother and he still ended up in prison. I prayed for my parents and they both deserted me and disappeared. I prayed to come home and when I finally got here, somebody tried to kill me."

"That's not God's fault. We're all responsible for the consequences of our personal choices."

She paused long enough to turn and speak over her shoulder. "Yeah, well, I choose to stand on my own two feet. I have since I was ten."

And that's about the saddest thing you've said so far, Shane concluded as he watched her work her way through the mob. If he and his mother had not had their faith to comfort and uphold them when his dad, Sheriff Sam Colton, had been killed, they might not have even survived, let alone made new lives for themselves.

Which reminded him. He needed to touch base with

his mom and Otis to fill them in before they learned the truth about Jamie from the town grapevine.

He smiled wryly. Given the speed of gossip in Serenity, it might already be too late.

Dropping back, Shane fisted his phone, pulled up her number and dialed. A familiar ringtone echoed from just across the street. Marsha had apparently left the beauty salon when she'd heard the ruckus and was now standing next to Jamie Lynn.

The call went to voice mail as Shane shoved his cell back in his pocket and headed toward them.

He was halfway there before he realized he didn't know whether he was on his way to inform Marsha who she was comforting or was simply eager to rejoin the attractive woman with the glitter of broken glass in her hair.

The fact that he had to ask himself that question in the first place was more disconcerting than the potential answer.

"Please," Jamie pleaded with the officer, "don't make me go to the hospital again. I needed treatment the last time but this is just superficial."

The deputy radioed information, listened, then nodded. "Okay. The chief says you can go. For now." His pencil was poised over a small notebook he'd pulled from his uniform shirt pocket. "What's your cell number and where are you staying?"

She recited her number, then pointed. "I'm at the Blue Jay motel, on the left past the stoplight."

"Got it." He handed back her driver's license. "Don't leave town."

The irony almost made Jamie laugh aloud. She let

herself grin at the young rookie. "You don't have to worry. I plan to stick around."

Marsha patted Jamie's arm. "Come home with us. I'll get that glass out of your hair for you and then we can share supper."

"No, really. I couldn't."

"Nonsense. Otis and I almost always have guests." She smiled at her son. "Shane and Kyle are regulars."

That comment hit Jamie so hard she reached for Shane's forearm and gripped tightly without thinking. "Kyle! Where is he? What did you do with him?"

"Relax. He's fine. I saw my pastor's wife coming out of the courthouse and dropped him off with her."

A lungful of air whooshed out, deflating Jamie like a cheap balloon. "Oh."

The look Shane was giving her was anything but amiable as he shook off her touch. "There was a time, just a few days ago, when I wouldn't have been afraid to leave him on a bench on the courthouse lawn all by himself. Then you showed up."

Marsha gasped. "Shane! What's gotten into you?"

"Her," he said with a shrug. "Has she told you who she is yet?"

Jamie Lynn was shaking her head. She hadn't intended to spread the news quite this fast but, given the present circumstances, she saw little reason to hedge. Instead, she offered her hand to the older woman. "My original name was Jamie Lynn *Henderson*. My brother is serving time for a crime he didn't commit."

"You're R.J.'s sister." It wasn't a query.

"Yes. I am."

As she watched, shock was replaced by an unexpected aura of peace that washed over Shane's mother and gave her a beatific appearance. She clasped Jamie's hand in both of hers. "I'm so sorry. That trial was a terrible ordeal—for all of us."

"Mother!"

Marsha eyed her son. "Oh, hush, Shane. This young woman wasn't involved. We can't choose who our relatives will be or control what they do."

Although Jamie Lynn didn't pull her hand away, she did say, "My brother's confession was coerced. He wasn't driving that night."

The disgusted noise Shane made needed no translation. Jamie Lynn looked into Marsha's misty blue gaze and said, "I'm just here to find the truth."

Behind her she heard Shane add, "No matter who it hurts."

"The truth can set us free," Marsha quoted. "Will you be able to accept it if you learn that your brother actually was guilty?"

"Of course." But would she? Jamie had believed so strongly that her well-loved sibling was innocent, she'd never considered finding evidence to the contrary. What if she did? What if their parents had been trying to protect them from worse emotional trauma by inventing the story about receiving criminal threats?

But if that were true, if the threats weren't real, then why send their daughter away? And why split up when Jamie knew how devoted to each other they had been?

No. There was a lot more to this puzzle, to this town, than met the eye. And one of the best places to start getting to the bottom of everything was by keeping company with someone who'd had a vested interest in the whole scenario, right from the start.

She smiled slightly, hoping Marsha was ready for

what she was about to say. "I'd like to take you up on your offer but now that you know exactly who I am, I'll understand if you want to withdraw your invitation."

"Nonsense. We'd love to have you."

"And I'd love to come," Jamie Lynn said, seeing Shane's face flush. It wasn't necessary to win him over or gain even partial cooperation. Marsha was the one who would know the most about the events surrounding the hit-and-run anyway. It was Marsha she needed to quiz.

Once again, her conscience reared its head, demanding attention. She reached for the older woman's hand. "You need to be aware that I intend to keep probing and asking questions until I get satisfactory answers."

"Fair enough." Marsha smiled, the outer corners of her eyes wrinkling to accent sparkling irises.

Those were Kyle's eyes, Jamie noted. The color reminded her of the ocean off the Atlantic coast; not exactly blue, not green, either, while Shane's were more like the afterglow of a sunset in the forest, all brown and gold.

Perhaps it wasn't the hues that made those people's eyes different, she mused. Perhaps it was the personalities behind their glances, particularly in the case of Marsha. Someone had taken her beloved husband from her, yet she was willing to befriend a stranger who she knew was kin to the convicted killer.

What kind of person could manage to do that? Jamie Lynn asked herself. The invitation was evidently genuine and came without strings attached.

Of course, it also meant she'd have to be around Shane for the rest of the evening. That, alone, should have shown her that she was getting in over her head, yet Jamie dismissed the notion. She knew what she was doing. A casual, frank conversation with the family of R.J.'s supposed victim was exactly what she needed as a base on which to build.

She gently touched her scalp with the tip of one finger, wondering how anybody was going to be able to remove all those tiny pieces of glass without scratching her or clogging up their plumbing.

When she glanced over at Shane, she apparently caught him off guard because, instead of the anger she'd expected, she thought she glimpsed empathy.

Then again, he had shown concern by trailing her even after he'd learned who she was. His approach was not nearly as gentle as Marsha's, of course. He had a macho image, not to mention a firm belief that his father's killer had been caught and punished. Naturally he would resist an alternate solution. Anybody would.

She pulled her gaze away from Shane and concentrated on his mother. "May Ulysses and I hitch a ride with you to the motel? I really should freshen up and change before supper."

"Of course."

Although Jamie Lynn didn't check Shane's reaction, she saw Marsha do just that, then smile and say, "You go fetch my grandson. We girls will meet you back at the house."

He huffed derisively. "Not on your life, Mom. Where that meddlesome woman goes, trouble follows. And so do I."

"Okay. Then meet us at the motel," Marsha said, looping her bent arm through Jamie's. Her smile widened. "Since you're so worried, I'll take Kyle home to play with Otis and you can give Jamie Lynn a ride to the house later, when she's ready."

Stuffing his hands into his pockets, Shane shrugged. "All right. We'll do it your way this time," he told Marsha. "Just don't forget who and what we're dealing with. Somebody has it in for Ms. Henderson—Nolan—but good, and they don't seem to have given up. Whenever you're with her, you can become collateral damage."

Hesitating, Jamie Lynn tugged on Marsha's arm. "Wait. This is a bad idea all the way around. Shane's right about people being after me. I don't want to do anything to put your family in jeopardy."

Marsha turned and clasped Jamie's free hand in both of hers. "Honey, I was married to Sam Colton for almost twenty years. During that time he received threats of all kinds. If I was ever worried about some good old boys heaving bricks through my windows, or some such nonsense, I got over it long ago."

"This could be a lot worse than a brick," Jamie Lynn warned.

"Nothing can ever be worse than losing my Sam," Marsha insisted. "When it's my time to go, it's my time. No human intervention can change that."

"You believe in fate?"

The older woman was shaking her head. Her eyes were so kind they tugged at Jamie's conscience even more.

"No. What I believe is that God loves me and has been looking after me since I was a child and first met Jesus." Her grip tightened. "What about you? What do you believe?"

"That I have to be responsible for my own life because nobody else is," Jamie said before thinking it through. When she saw pity in Marsha's expression, she wished she'd chosen her words with more care.

Instead of commenting, however, Marsha merely turned and led her toward a newer white sedan. A click of a key fob unlocked the doors remotely and made the lights flash.

Jamie circled, passed her little dog across to Marsha, then sat sideways on the edge of the passenger seat and bent forward over the curbside to shake loose glass out of her hair.

Satisfied she'd done all she could, she swung her legs in, pulled Ulysses onto her lap and slammed the door. She desperately wanted to explain what she'd meant when she'd said that nobody else cared what became of her, but the right words failed to materialize. Aunt Tessie cared, yes. As for anyone else, who knew? Certainly not Jamie Lynn.

By the time Shane located Kyle and made suitable excuses to the gang of church ladies who had gathered to bemoan the fact that he'd passed his child off so easily, Marsha's car had left the square. Since he already knew where she was headed and how close the cozy motel was to the middle of Serenity, he wasn't worried about safety. The idiots who had taken a potshot at Jamie Lynn were bound to know better than to try anything else right away, particularly with the square swarming with cops.

He smiled, realizing that the Serenity version of a swarm of police was far different from a city show of force. Nevertheless, there were enough cops present to ensure that whoever had been targeting the Henderson/Nolan woman would be long gone. Good ole boys might be wild and rowdy but they weren't stupid. They were, for the most part, endowed with the innate savvy of natural hunters and fishermen, particularly since that kind of outdoor activity was such a big part of their upbringing.

Even he could shoot well, Shane reminded himself. His dad had seen to that long ago. With Sam's careful instruction had come safety lessons, too. Guns didn't worry Shane except for Kyle's presence in the home, so he kept the firearms separate from the ammo and locked each component in a different cabinet.

It occurred to him that perhaps he should ask his mother about his dad's old service revolver. As long as there was a threat of violence, it would do his mom well to know where the weapon was and how to properly load it.

Kyle spotted his grandmother first. She was standing in front of the motel office as they came to a stop.

"Memaw!"

"That's right, buddy. You're going home with her and I'm coming later. Okay?"

"I wanna go see the doggie again."

Shane heaved a sigh. "You will. He's coming to Memaw and Otis's for supper tonight."

"Hooray!"

Yeah, big whoop, Shane thought as he unfastened his son's safety belt and helped him out.

The child made a dash for Marsha. She bent to hug him, then straightened to speak to Shane. "Jamie's in 6-B, down this first hallway."

"Why tell me? I'm waiting right out here."

"I know. That's what I told her. I..." She scowled. "I'm just worried about her, that's all."

"You have too soft a heart, Mom."

"Don't give me that much credit, honey. When she first told me who she was, I didn't have very Christian thoughts."

"Yeah, well, I still don't." He spoke quietly, leaning closer. "Be very careful what you tell her. She can be trouble. She's already caused plenty."

"Is that her fault?" Marsha asked. "I mean, all she's doing is asking questions about why her brother was sent to prison. If there's nothing wrong with his conviction, why does it look like somebody's really upset with her? Maybe she's onto something."

Shane's eyebrows arched. "Are you serious? How can you even think of anybody reopening Dad's case? Didn't it hurt enough fourteen years ago?"

The look in his mother's eyes and the slight droop of her shoulders told him he'd overstepped. "I'm sorry. I just don't want you to have to go through all that misery again."

"It won't be the same," Marsha explained. "*I'm* not the same. It's hard to explain. All I can say is that your father's death affected me in ways I hadn't anticipated."

"You did seem to take it better than I'd expected."

She smiled slightly and nodded. "I had my moments. Still do. Once in a while, some thought or outside trigger will set me off and I can't stop crying."

"You never told me that."

"Of course not. You had your own grief when you were younger, and then your marriage crashed. Why would I add worry about my crazy feelings if I didn't have to?"

"Because I care?"

"Of course you do. I still miss your dad every day,

yet I know it's foolish to grieve the way I did when he first left this world."

"Which is why you're okay with that woman digging up the past?"

"That's part of it." Shane saw her countenance harden. "The other part is personal. I want to know who killed my Sam as much as she does."

"We *know* who did it."

"Do we?" Her head tilted and her eyes narrowed. "If Sam had been able to investigate that hit-and-run himself, I wonder who he'd have arrested."

FIVE

Jamie Lynn managed to shampoo the last tiny shards out of her hair, then gave it a careful combing. That was one good thing about safety glass. It broke into pieces that didn't have very sharp edges.

Glad to be back in her own clothing, she smoothed the hem of her red T-top over the hips of white linen slacks and slipped into her sandals. Although the spring day had been warm, she expected a cooler evening so she grabbed a light sweater.

Ulysses began to dance at the door when he saw her pick up her shoulder bag.

"Yes, you get to go," she said with a smile. "And play with that nice little boy again."

Truth to tell, she wished she were headed for a pleasant evening of socialization instead of an inquest. Marsha was a lovely person. And the child was darling.

Jamie set her jaw. His daddy wasn't bad, either, once you got past the chip on his shoulder. Before he'd learned her identity, he'd been pleasant. Tender. Even joyful, particularly when he'd gone out of his way to catch and look after Useless-Ulysses. The mistake took her by surprise. Made her shake her head and grin.

That man had gotten under her skin, all right. It would be nice if his current presence didn't feel like a touch of poison ivy.

Still smiling and thinking about rejoining Shane in the parking lot, she scooped up her little dog, tucked him under one arm and pulled the door to her room shut with a bang.

Ulysses stilled. The beginning of a growl made his tiny body vibrate.

Jamie Lynn froze. Listened. Waited to see what her pet sensed that she had missed noticing.

The nape of her neck prickled. Goose bumps tingled along her arms and a shiver traced her spine. She was not alone.

Slowly swiveling her neck, she glimpsed movement out of the corner of her eye. Before she could get a better look, a meaty hand clamped over her mouth and a deep voice rumbled, "Don't make a sound."

At that point the command was unnecessary because Jamie's voice failed her. Simply drawing breath was hard enough. Fear paralyzed her. Stole strength from her limbs and thoughts from her mind.

"You need to leave town," the man ordered.

His mouth was so close to her ear she could feel his hot breath on her cheek and smell alcohol. That was how her brother had smelled all too often in his late teens, another reason why he'd been a prime suspect for the fatal hit-and-run.

Remembering R.J. was enough stimulus to raise Jamie Lynn's ire. She stiffened. Tried to break free.

The man's grip tightened, pinching her face.

She began to make noise, a whine growing louder behind her closed lips.

His "Shut up!" was menacing and then some.

That was apparently enough to set off Ulysses because the little dog's growl became a fierce bark.

The attacker loosened his grip on Jamie to reach for the dog and was rewarded by a bite. Cursing, he shook his bleeding hand and took a step backward.

Jamie unleashed a scream that rattled the windows in the exterior hallway. She bolted, shrieking as she ran.

By the time she reached the end of the hall, she was almost as breathless as she'd been after the fire.

Someone grabbed her. She swung her purse and connected with a thunk.

"Hey. Cut it out. It's me!"

She had to blink repeatedly to focus on Shane and take in her new reality. All she could do was point and stammer, "He, he…"

Shane tried to set her aside. "No! Don't leave me."

Although every fiber of Shane's being wanted to give chase to whoever had frightened her, he heeded her panicky request. "All right. Tell me what happened."

"A man. Outside my room. He grabbed me."

"Did he hurt you?" Shane studied her face. "It looks like he slapped your cheek."

"No. He held his hand over my mouth really tightly and it pinched."

"Did he say anything?"

Shane saw her dark eyes widen as she looked into his. "Yes. He told me to leave town!"

"All right. We're calling the police."

"Again? They're going to think I'm looking for attention if I keep having to involve them."

"Would you rather let whoever is doing this get away with it?"

"Of course not."

He could tell that she was starting to regain her self-control because she'd released the fistful of his jacket fabric and started to ease away, blushing so brightly the injury to her face almost disappeared.

Urging her into the motel office, he told the clerk to call 911, then started back outside.

Jamie Lynn made a grab at his sleeve. "Where are you going?"

"To look for clues."

"Don't you think that's best left to the professionals?"

"My dad taught me how to behave around a crime scene. Where, exactly, were you when the guy grabbed you?"

"Right outside my room."

"6-B?"

"Yes."

"Had you stepped away from the door?"

"I'd turned around to check the lock. You know, jiggle the knob to make sure the door was locked. That's when Ulysses started to growl."

"Good. Anything else?"

"Yes!" The excitement in that single word gave him added hope.

"What did you just remember?" Shane asked.

Jamie Lynn began hugging and petting the dog she still held tucked under one arm. "Ulysses bit him!"

She directed lavish praise on her faithful pet and began to coo, "What a good little boy you are. Yes, you are. A sweet, sweet boy."

"Did he draw blood?"

"What?"

"Blood. Is there a chance the dog's teeth broke the skin? Or was the man wearing gloves?"

"Um, I don't think I felt gloves. It all happened so fast I'm not totally positive."

"All right. In that case I'll wait for a deputy. I wouldn't want to step on the only drop of blood left behind and ruin evidence."

"Shouldn't you phone your mother and tell her we'll be late for supper?"

"You're still going? Even after this?" The incredulous look she sent his way provided the answer before she spoke. He clenched his jaw.

"Of course I'm going. I meant what I told you and Marsha. I'm not going to let anybody scare me off. If they'd wanted to kill me they could have done it a few minutes ago and you wouldn't have suspected a thing until you got tired of waiting and came looking for me."

"That's probably a valid argument."

"Of course it is. Now that I've had time to think about it, I doubt that the fire was meant to be fatal, either. When they couldn't find me inside, I think they assumed I'd escaped and torched the house to cover their tracks."

"What about the shooting in front of the old police station?"

"They missed me then, too."

"Because it's hard to fire accurately from a moving vehicle," Shane argued. "That truck was speeding so fast it almost turned over when it skidded around the corner."

"Meaning, you believe I'm in real danger?"

He rolled his eyes as he drawled, "Well, yeah."

"Opinion noted," Jamie Lynn said. She pointed toward the street. "Looks like the cavalry is here. If I get to know these officers any better, I'm going to have to start baking them cookies."

Facing her, Shane grasped her upper arms. "Will you at least try to look scared, the way you did when you came running to me, so they'll take you seriously?"

"I wasn't running to you. I was running from the other guy."

He was taken aback when she set Ulysses on the ground at her feet, straightened and held out her hands. Tremors in her fingers gave her away. She put on a good act, but beneath the unruffled exterior she was still plenty terrified.

Shane wasn't sure whether to be glad she was wary or sorry for her. Either way, at least he knew that inside, where it really counted, she wasn't nearly as hard-boiled as she pretended to be.

This police officer was new to her. At least Jamie Lynn thought he was. Except for Sheriff Allgood, who was considerably older, the men's faces were beginning to look alike to her. So was their skepticism. Bidding this particular officer goodbye, she sighed, shook her head and made a face at Shane. "That went about as well as I'd figured it would."

"At least he took your statement."

"Yes, and promised to send someone to look for drops of blood in the hall. Do you think he will?"

"I have my doubts."

"Then we should try."

Shane didn't seem particularly happy about the prospect of turning amateur CSI. "My success will be iffy,

at best. The problem is collecting a sample without con-
taminating it."

He looked to Sadie, the motel's owner, a rotund,
motherly-looking woman he'd known since childhood.
"Do you have a plastic sandwich bag that's never been
opened?"

"Sure do. If you can prove who's been harassing my
guests, I'll give you anything you ask for."

"The bag will be enough," Shane replied. "Just be
sure the seal at the top is closed, just the way it came
out of the box."

"Gotcha. Hang on. Be right back."

"How will that help?" Jamie asked. Confused, she
was glad Shane had taken charge because she was
clearly in over her head in this instance.

"Coming from the factory, it should be sanitary
enough to store a clean sample. Providing we locate
one, that is."

Sadie breezed back to the counter and produced the
plastic bag he'd asked for. "Here you go. Need a flashlight?"

"That would be helpful, yes." Shane turned to Jamie
and pointed to her dog. "Carry him. We don't want him
spoiling the evidence."

"Right." Although she did as told, she hesitated inside the motel lobby.

"You have to come with me," Shane reminded her.
"Otherwise I may search all night and not even be looking in the right place."

"I understand. It's just that…"

When he turned his full attention to her, she felt
the effect of his inner strength as well as saw his determination.

"I'm licensed to carry a concealed weapon," Shane told her. "We won't be walking into this unarmed, if that's what you're worried about."

"It had occurred to me." Holding her wiggling dog closer, she said, "Okay. Let's go."

As anticipated, the hallway was cloaked in shadow. The setting sun shone on a few tiny sections of it, throwing the rest into darkness by comparison. Taking her place at Shane's shoulder, she pointed. "My room is just past that big potted plant. If there is any blood, it has to be on the other side."

"When you ran, did he follow?"

"I—I don't think so." She dropped back one step, no more. There was something terribly comforting about being with Shane Colton in spite of his rigid conclusions about her brother. She supposed, under the same circumstances, she wouldn't be very open to stirring things up, either.

That sensible conclusion helped settle her mind a bit, although her body continued to tremble.

Ulysses's growl vibrated against her chest and tingled her fingers.

She touched Shane's shoulder. "Wait. Stop."

"What's wrong?"

"The dog is growling again. He did the same thing just before I was grabbed."

Flashlight in one hand, Shane slipped a .38 automatic from a holster inside his belt and stood ready. "Get behind me. Against the wall."

She watched from there as he played the beam of light over the entire area, finding nothing.

"Useless is probably remembering the last time,"

Shane said, illuminating the pavement next. "This has to be the right place."

"More to the left," Jamie Lynn told him. "Yes! There."

He crouched, inverted the bag and touched it to a dot on the ground before righting it and zipping it closed. "There was more than one drop still wet so I chose the smallest. That will leave plenty for crime scene investigating if they ever send anybody by to look."

"What do we do with that?" Jamie asked.

"Deliver it to Harlan and call in a favor." Shane holstered his gun, then cupped her elbow. "Come on. We'll drop this by the sheriff's office on our way to supper."

"Oh, dear. I'd forgotten all about that. Your poor mom must be worried sick."

Shane frowned. "You suggested I phone her, so I did."

It occurred to Jamie that her unplanned contact with the Colton family was an extraordinary coincidence. Aunt Tessie would have given credit to God, of course. She always thanked Him, even when things didn't work out the way she wanted. A sense of peace usually followed, too, at least in regard to Tessie. There had been many times when Jamie Lynn had envied her aunt's faith.

There had also been times when she had wondered how anybody could continue to trust God when so many things went so very wrong, such as R.J.'s unjust conviction.

Everyone in her family had prayed fervently for the truth to come out, yet an innocent young man had been sent to prison and remained there. A righteous God wouldn't have let that happen, would He?

Following Shane to his truck and climbing in, Jamie Lynn mulled over her original reasons for returning to a town she'd thought she hated. There were nice folks here. Helpful, caring people such as Sadie and Marsha. And even Shane.

Truth to tell, it was a big step for him to set aside his prejudices and reach out to help her through this maze of confusion and apparent danger. He might cause her untold trouble in the future when she dug into the evidence surrounding the hit-and-run, but right now he was going out of his way to provide aid. As far as she was concerned, that made him a hero.

She petted the dog in her lap and began to smile as she carried that notion further and envisioned Shane dressed as a superhero. He'd be handsome, of course, and strong, but in his case his costume was denim and his cape slightly wrinkled. Which would make for a bumpy flight, she concluded.

"Why are you grinning like that?" he asked.

"Maybe I'm just glad you were there when I needed you and able to find a blood sample," she said.

He huffed cynically. "If I believed for a second that that was the only notion bouncing around in your brain, I wouldn't be nearly so worried."

When she glanced at him and saw how deeply he was scowling, it was all Jamie could do to keep from laughing out loud.

SIX

Shane was not surprised to find that the normally casual atmosphere at Marsha and Otis's was noticeably altered. Only Kyle seemed oblivious to any difference, and that was mostly due to his infatuation with Useless. Marsha bustled from kitchen to dinner table and back far more than usual, Otis seemed at a loss for relevant conversation and Shane, himself, was determined to protect his family's feelings no matter what. That made for an atmosphere so strained it was almost palpable.

It didn't help when Jamie remarked, "I'm sorry we were delayed. We had to wait for the police again."

Shane rescued a bowl of steaming potatoes from his mother's hands and set it on a trivet. "Everything's okay. No harm was done this time."

"Jamie? Are you all right?" the tenderhearted woman asked.

"She's fine." Shane took his own regular seat across from their guest, unfolding his son's napkin and tucking it under the boy's chin.

When he looked up again, his mother was glaring at him. "Why didn't you tell me that when you called?"

"Because I didn't want to worry you. Like now," he

said with an arch of his eyebrows. "There's no reason to get upset."

One quick glance at Jamie Lynn told him otherwise. Nevertheless, he saw her manage a smile for his mother.

"It turned out to be a good thing Shane decided to be the one to wait for me at the motel," Jamie said. "Knowing he was nearby probably scared off the thug."

"What's a tug?" Kyle piped up.

"A thug is a bad guy," she explained.

"Like an ogre?"

Shane noticed her eyes beginning to sparkle with what he assumed was mirth.

"A bad ogre, maybe. Not the nice cartoon kind." She took a helping of potatoes, then passed the bowl. "You know about being careful to not talk to strangers, don't you?"

The child's head bobbed. "Uh-huh. Memaw told me. Stranger danger."

"That's right."

Kyle suddenly sobered. "Are you a stranger?"

"Not really." Jamie's smile gentled. So did her eyes. "But you still need to listen to your daddy and the rest of your family if they tell you to stay away from somebody, even me. I wouldn't want anything bad to happen to such a good buddy of Useless."

The five-year-old clapped his hands and grinned. "See, Memaw? I told you that was his name."

The soft laugh Shane heard coming from Jamie was so congenial, so comfortable, he was taken aback. Apparently, interacting with children was her gift and doing so allowed her to relax and be herself. Too bad adults were so perceptive. There was no way he'd ever be able to think of her as anything but a poser, a liar who pretended to be someone else so she could return to Serenity and begin digging up dirt on people he called his friends.

That was part of the problem, he realized. A big part.

Shane clamped his jaw tight as reality dawned. To take her accusations seriously would mean looking beneath the surface of dozens of lives that up until now had seemed untainted. Honest. Not only acceptable but exemplary. He didn't want to see any of their reputations torn down or tainted, especially not by baseless rumors.

Looking at her across the dining table and appreciating her tenderness and beauty the way he had been when she was talking with his son, it was easy for Shane to forget how dangerous she was to his family's stability, not to mention the unidentified menace that might be watching her every move.

Jamie offered to help Marsha clear the table and do the dishes. Her motive was not totally unselfish. One, she wanted to escape the tension in the dining room, and, two, she wanted the chance to quiz Sam's widow in private. To her delight and relief, Marsha expressed a similar desire.

"I'll rinse and load the dishwasher while you hand me the plates and fill me in on what made you decide to come back," the older woman said. "And don't be like Shane."

"Like Shane? How?"

"He tries to protect me. Always has, particularly since Sam was killed." She grew pensive, her hands stilling. "It's funny. My life is divided into two parts, the years before Sam was taken from me and the years since, almost like I'm two different people."

Jamie Lynn nodded soberly. "I know what you mean. Until I saw Serenity again, I felt as if the girl I'd been before I went to live with Aunt Tessie was just a fantasy."

"Whatever happened to your parents?"

"I wish I knew. That's one of the reasons I'm here. Tessie finally gave me some details about my past and the more I thought about it, the more I wanted to know the whole truth."

Marsha had gone back to scraping and rinsing plates. "Why didn't you just ask your aunt?"

"I did. She insisted she didn't know anything else. After R.J. was arrested and went to trial, Mom sent me to Tessie's. I thought she was just trying to shield me during the trial. I had no idea I was staying for good."

"That must have been hard on all of you."

"Yes. I'm afraid I made everybody's life miserable for a while. I was mad at the world."

"What happened next?"

"Dad soon left Mom and everybody seemed to accept it as desertion. However, according to Tessie, both my parents had been threatened with harm if they kept trying to prove R.J. was innocent. After Dad disappeared and she knew I was safe with my aunt in New England, Mom supposedly left everything behind and hit the road—for her own protection."

"And you *believe* that?" Marsha looked astounded.

"I was a lot more skeptical until I got here and met with such violent resistance to my queries."

Silent for a moment, Jamie Lynn mulled over the events of the past few days. "You know, if whoever is upset about my interest in the past would have left me alone, I'd probably have satisfied my curiosity as best I could and gone back to New England none the wiser."

"And now?"

She huffed and shook her head. "Now? Now they couldn't get rid of me with dynamite."

Marsha quirked a smile. "Let's pray they don't go that far. From what my son has told me, it sounds as if they were just trying to scare you off. So, what's plan B?"

Jamie shrugged. "Beats me. I've requested copies of the trial transcripts and I plan to try to look up some of my brother's friends from his teen years, if they're still around. Other than that, I have no idea."

"Maybe I can help you."

"Really? You'd do that? For me?"

"For you, and to get justice for my Sam. That is your goal, isn't it?"

"Yes!"

"Then let's finish up these dishes and go talk to Shane."

That suggestion dampened Jamie's enthusiasm the way a bucket of ice water being dumped over her head would have. "He's not exactly in my corner, if you know what I mean."

"I do, and it saddens me." Marsha smiled, clearly lost in thought for a moment. "I had hoped I'd raised him better."

"He had a traumatic childhood," Jamie Lynn offered. "We both did. Things like that can affect people their entire lives, whether they recognize the negative influence or not."

"I know. Right now it's Kyle who worries me most. I do the best I can but he needs a mother."

Curiosity made Jamie ask, "What happened to Shane's marriage?"

"After Kyle was born, Roz decided she preferred the single life over being a wife and mother. Shane was devastated when she left them."

"I can imagine. Tessie became my lifeline after my family fell apart," Jamie told her. "I still miss Mom, but when I have fond memories of growing up they usually center on my great-aunt—great in more ways than one. She was a lot older than my parents, yet she's never failed to love and encourage me. That's what kids need most. I told Shane the same thing this afternoon. Remember?"

"Yes, I do. I think that was when you won me over." Drying her hands on a dish towel, she said, "Let's get going. I want to catch Shane while he's in a good mood."

As long as one member of the Colton family was on her side, that was enough—and more than she had hoped for.

As she rinsed and dried her hands, hung the damp towel next to the sink and followed Marsha, she grew more and more unsettled. *Strange.* If she didn't know better she might suspect it was being near Shane that had her so agitated, rather than the expectation of difficulty in clearing her innocent brother. That was ridiculous, of course.

And yet, a little voice in the back of her mind kept reminding her that the man who supposedly didn't even *like* her had repeatedly come to her rescue.

Saving her life by dragging her out of a burning building wasn't exactly a small thing, was it? Nor was the physical protection he'd been providing since then. If she were totally honest with herself, she would have to admit that she had begun viewing him as her anchor, her stronghold. A haven to seek when fear threatened to overwhelm her.

Looking past Marsha, she studied Shane as they entered the living room. His brief glance passed over his mother first, then drifted to her. Their gazes locked as if welded together. Where Jamie Lynn had expected animosity, or at the very least, discontent, she found something else. Something almost tender.

Be sensible. He's been playing with Kyle and my dog so of course he looks happier, she told herself.

Unfortunately, that conclusion didn't begin to explain why *she* was so happy to see *him.*

Shane had no trouble reading his mother's expression. She was up to something. What the Henderson woman was thinking, however, remained a puzzle. How she could look so appealing and off-putting at the same time was driving him crazy.

He left Kyle sitting on the floor, petting Useless, and got to his feet to face them. "What?"

"Don't scowl at me like that," his mother said. "We just need a little favor."

"Uh-huh." He crossed his arms on his chest and stood firm, feet slightly apart to complete the image. "Like what? Should I brave gunfire and battle criminals again? Or did you have something a tad less dangerous in mind?"

"This is safe. Definitely safe," Marsha told him with a grin. "Remember all those boxes of your father's that you stored for me when I married Otis and moved over here?"

Shane regarded her with caution. "Yes…"

"Well, I need them. At least I need some of them, and since I can't be sure which is which, I'd like you to bring them all to me."

"Why?" When he glanced back at Jamie, he realized she didn't know, either.

"Because I want to look at Sam's old notebooks, particularly the ones from the period right before he was killed," Marsha explained.

"What good will that do? It'll just upset you."

"If it does, it does," she replied decisively. "While Jamie Lynn was telling me about her parents receiving threats, it occurred to me that your dad had, too."

"That's not news."

"No, but perhaps the timing of them is. All these years we've believed Sam was killed by a drunk driver. What if the whole incident was set up to look that way? What if he was actually lured out onto that dark, deserted road so he could be murdered?"

Shane realized he was gaping and that he wasn't the only one who was astonished. Even poor Otis looked perplexed.

"There was no indication of that," Shane said. "None. It was just a hit-and-run. Everybody agreed."

"Yes, they did," Jamie said, stepping up beside the older woman. "But they also agreed that my brother was the driver of the car that hit him. What if that really was a frame job? And suppose my father was gotten out of the way, like my aunt thinks he was, before my mother ran away to save herself?"

"That's ridiculous."

"Then prove it. To both of us," Jamie said, reaching for Marsha's hand and giving it a squeeze of encouragement before she added, "And to yourself."

"I don't find it necessary to prove anything to myself, Ms. Henderson, or Nolan, or whatever name you choose to use for convenience. I was beginning to think you were going to be reasonable about all this."

"I am being reasonable. I didn't even know your father left behind notebooks until now, so I certainly couldn't have coerced your mother into asking for them."

"So you claim."

"I don't lie."

Shane stood firm, wondering what it would take to win their argument. "Neither do I."

"Fine. Then get the storage boxes."

"I'm not sure where they are."

The second he spoke he suspected he had just lost their current battle of wits. When Jamie Lynn began to smile at him, he was certain.

"Really?" she asked. "I thought you didn't lie."

"I don't."

"You mean you don't *usually*, right?"

Shane uncrossed his arms, hooked his thumbs in his jeans pockets and struck what he hoped was a casual pose. "Sometimes a small fib is necessary in order to look after those we care about."

"Ri-i-i-ight."

Not only were her dark eyes sparkling, she was clearly enjoying his mistake. Well, too bad. He was sticking to his first reaction. Handing over those notebooks would be the worst thing he could do for his mother. He'd looked after her for years, before she'd married again, and he didn't intend to do anything that would hurt her now.

A chuckle came from the largest recliner in the living

room, drawing everyone's attention. Otis was not only laughing, he began to applaud. "Good one, Jamie girl."

"Thank you. I try."

Shane glared at his stepfather but refrained from comment. After all, Mom loved the guy, and Otis wasn't a bad choice as a pleasant companion for her twilight years. It was the old man's odd sense of humor that sometimes went too far. Like now.

Chuckling again, Otis waggled his bushy gray eyebrows. "Don't bother giving me a dirty look, son. Just see that you remember this conversation the first time you catch our boy in a whopper."

Realizing that Kyle was paying close attention to the adults while grinning at his papaw, Shane backed down. "You're right. Since I don't want my son to lie, I'd better set a good example. I think I can locate those boxes of Dad's things if you'll give me a couple of days. They're probably buried under piles of other stuff in the back of my barn."

Everyone was grinning except him. And with good reason. Not only was he hesitant to dig out the old handwritten notes, he loathed reading them. His mother wasn't the only one who had relegated her memories of the late sheriff to the past.

Shane had lost more than his father when Sam had died.

He'd lost his only hero.

SEVEN

Jamie hated to be idle for an hour, let alone days. Quiet time gave her too much opportunity to remember how much she missed the kids she'd worked with in preschool before taking this leave of absence to sort out her family's troubles.

As soon as her truck was ready, she picked it up and drove straight to the courthouse, marching directly to the clerk's office.

"Hello," Jamie said with a smile. "I phoned a few weeks ago about getting some old records of the Henderson trial. My name is Nolan."

"I'll need to see some identification," the pleasant, middle-aged woman said. "Since I don't know you, I mean. Usually, the folks who come to us are locals."

"I used to be," Jamie told her, producing her driver's license. It had occurred to her to keep her real identity as secret as possible, but she quickly rationalized that the people who already knew who she was were the only ones she needed to fear.

She held out her hand for the manila envelope the other woman had produced from under the counter. "My name was Henderson when I lived in Serenity. Jamie Lynn Henderson."

To her credit, the clerk's gasp was inaudible. "Oh, my. I see. Well, we charge ten cents a page. The total is—" she pointed "—right here. Will this be cash or check?"

"Cash, but I suppose I should ask for a receipt."

"All righty, coming up." The woman's hands were slightly unsteady as she filled out the slip, signed it and took the money. "So, what brings you…" Blushing, she stopped herself and eyed the bulky envelope. "Silly me. You're here to learn all about the trial. I can understand wanting to trace your roots."

"Did you know my family well?"

"The Hendersons? Not really. They lived pretty far out of town and I was a city girl."

"You didn't even know my mother, Alice?"

The clerk blanched. "Alice was your mother? I don't recall a daughter Jamie."

"My family always called me Baby Sister. I imagine the only ones who knew my name were my teachers and the kids at school."

"I see." Her glance darted to the envelope. "Then R.J. was your brother." She reached to pat Jamie's hand. "I'm so sorry, dear."

This show of compassion was a surprise. "Thank you."

"We could have mailed those copies, you know. Saved you a trip from… I didn't notice when I looked at your license."

"New England. Rhode Island, specifically. I've lived there for years. Ever since the trial."

"Too bad it ended the way it did." She was slowly shaking her head and her eyes held a faraway look. "I used to go upstairs to the courtroom on my breaks and watch the proceedings. Surprised me, I'll tell you, when that poor boy went to jail."

Jamie stiffened. "Why is that?"

"Oh, I don't know. He just seemed so lost, as if he'd given up hope. I'd have thought anybody who was facing a manslaughter charge would have tried harder to fight against conviction."

"I agree," Jamie told her. "I think he was framed."

"But—he admitted it."

"Yes. The question is, why did he wait so long and what finally convinced him to change his plea?"

"Maybe his conscience bothered him."

"Maybe." Jamie Lynn was nodding slowly, thoughtfully. "And maybe somebody scared him enough to make him take the blame for something he didn't do."

Leaving the astonished clerk, she wheeled and headed for the door. The way she saw it, there were two ways to approach the gossip grapevine. She could either try to avoid becoming the subject of everyone's interest, or she could take advantage of the rapid spread of rumor and see if it rattled any cages or turned up more evidence. Anybody who was on her side might contact her if it got out that she was in town on her brother's behalf.

And, as she had already found out, anybody who didn't want the truth exposed would try to scare her off. What they didn't know was how determined she was and that she was learning how truly brave she could be.

She hugged the envelope to her as she approached her truck. Above all, she hoped that reading these records wouldn't destroy her fond image of a caring, innocent sibling.

Logic insisted that that was a possibility.

Love for R.J. denied it.

* * *

Shane was not a happy camper. Not in the least. But a promise was a promise. He'd already put this off for several days. It was time to root out the storage boxes his mother had asked for, dust them off and load them into his truck.

He was on his way to the barn when his cell rang. "You're up early, Mom."

"I wanted to catch you before you went to work."

"Is something wrong?"

"Nope. Just wondering if you'd had a chance to look for your dad's papers yet."

"I was on my way to do that when you called." Shane heard her chuckle. "Well, I was."

"Okay. I believe you. Have you heard anything from Jamie Lynn?"

"Not since she picked up her truck, and we didn't talk much then." That lack of camaraderie had bothered him some, although it was exactly what he kept insisting he wanted. Go figure. "Why?"

Marsha sounded as if she was smiling as she said, "Well, in case you care, I have. She picked up the trial transcripts yesterday and hasn't had any more trouble."

"I suppose that's a plus." What might happen when the nosy young woman got her hands on the sheriff's private files, compliments of his mother, was a different story. One that gave him chills.

That unpleasant reaction helped Shane choose his next step—a delaying tactic. "Listen, Mom, I'll haul whatever I find to my garage in town so I can blow the dust off before you take any of it into your house. You know how allergic you get. Those boxes have to be covered with years of pollen and dirt."

"All right. Since it's Saturday and you close early, why not plan on bringing them to me as soon as you're free? And staying for supper, of course."

That was *not* what Shane wanted to do, for several reasons, the most important being his desire to censor what she read. "I'll see. You know how the repair business is. Farmers always break equipment right in the middle of a project and need it working ASAP."

"Murphy's Law," Marsha said. "Okay. Do the best you can. I'm glad you got Jamie Lynn's truck fixed. She really wanted her wheels back."

"And I wanted her to stop hanging around the garage," Shane admitted. "She was about to drive me crazy."

"Only because of the tires?" Marsha teased.

"Yes." He hoped he sounded as adamant as he'd intended. The last thing he needed was to give his mother more fodder for her romantic interpretations of inconsequential events. "*Only* because of the tires."

"Okay, if you say so."

"Look, Mom, if I don't get a move on I'm not going to have time to hunt up Dad's files this morning."

"Okay. Hug Kyle for me and tell him I'm looking forward to seeing him later."

"Right. Bye."

Shane checked his watch. Kyle would probably sleep for another hour, at least. If he hurried he might be able to get all the boxes loaded before it was time to wake him.

Yes, he knew exactly where the papers were stored.

And, no, he did not want to give them to his mother when he was positive they would cause her renewed pain.

But what choice did he have? They were technically her property and she was entitled to them.

Eventually.
After he'd sorted the contents.

Jamie had spent most of her time reading her brother's file. If it hadn't been for needing to walk the dog and find something to eat, she might not have ventured out at all. Most of the trial transcript was pretty boring and repetitive. Highlighting the interesting parts had made it much easier to remember where they were and revisit them to make notes.

One thing she was finding disturbing was the lack of input from R.J. It was as if he had been relegated to the role of mute observer while his future was stolen and his life ruined. At times, the attorney who was supposed to represent the Hendersons sounded as if he worked for the prosecution.

And the judge was just as opinionated and stern. R.J. had recanted his initial, unofficial confession and pleaded innocent as the trial began. Later, his lawyer had requested a private audience with the judge and had officially switched his plea to guilty.

The jury was summarily dismissed and the proceedings wrapped up quickly. Since R.J. was being tried as an adult and his crime was against a well-liked sheriff, he received a stiff penalty: thirty years.

She pushed the file away, weary and confused. Looking up the number in a phone book as thin as a cheap pulp magazine, she dialed Marsha Colton Bryce.

"Hello! Did you change your mind?"

Jamie paused and frowned. "I beg your pardon?"

"Oops. I didn't look at the number. I thought you were Shane."

"Is everything okay with you?" Still worried about

her enemies spreading their evil to her new acquaintances, she felt a catch in her throat.

"Fine. Or, as Otis likes to say, 'Finer than frog hair.'"

"There's no problem? You haven't been threatened or anything?"

"Of course not. Besides, Sam taught me to defend myself and I kept in practice all those years I was single. Nobody better mess with this pistol-packin' granny."

Her Wild West attitude amused Jamie Lynn. "Good for you. I might like to learn to shoot if the laws weren't so strict where I'm from."

"You just need to watch that you don't go off half-cocked, as they used to say when pistols and long guns were flintlocks."

"That's where that old saying came from?"

"Sure is." Marsha was chuckling. "So, what can I do for you? Did you get the trial transcripts read?"

"Yes. I stayed up half the night and I'm more confused than before. Has Shane brought you Sam's notes yet?"

"No, but he's due here later today and should have everything with him. He was getting the boxes loaded in his truck when I spoke to him about a half hour ago."

"That's wonderful." Uncertain how to politely invite herself back to Marsha's home, Jamie paused.

"How would you like to stop by for supper?" Marsha asked.

"Really? Could I? I don't want to cause any trouble."

There was still a hint of mirth in Marsha's voice when she said, "Honey, I think it's a tad late to worry about that. You just come. I'll handle my son."

"I—I meant with whoever was stalking me."

"I know you did." She chuckled softly. "Shane will blow a gasket when he figures it all out."

"Figures what out?"

"That I plan to do everything I can to help you find the truth. Between the two of us, and with the help of the good Lord, I think we can solve the puzzle, don't you?"

Relief at not having to stand alone against unknown enemies washed over Jamie Lynn.

All she could manage to say was, "Thank you."

Dusting the tops of the cardboard boxes with an open hand, Shane opened one and paused. There was no reason to look in the notebooks or file folders that lay before him. No reason at all.

"Except that I need to sort this material before I give it to Mom," he muttered. If he doled out the records one box at a time, he'd have enough spare time to read ahead and examine the notebooks.

A shrill voice came from the direction of the house. "Daddy? Where are you?"

The child came out onto the back porch. His curly hair was tousled and he was rubbing sleep out of his eyes.

"I'm right here, Kyle. Go get dressed. I'll be in to fix you breakfast in a minute."

Instead of obeying, the barefoot little boy joined his daddy. "Whatcha doin'?"

"Getting some old stuff for your memaw."

"Why?"

"Because she asked me to."

"Oh. Why?"

Shane couldn't help smiling. Once one of Kyle's inquisitions started there was no telling how long it would last. "Because she wants it." Before the child had a chance to ask more he said, "I thought I told you to get dressed."

"Uh-huh. Is it a school day?"

"No, it's Saturday, You don't have to wear your good clothes but pick something nice. We're going to take these boxes to Memaw later."

"Aw right!" Whirling, he started for the house.

Shane's heart swelled, thankful for what he had and reminded of what he'd lost. He'd given Roz all the love he could, yet it had not been enough. She'd already begun expressing restlessness when her unexpected pregnancy had made matters worse. She'd argued for terminating it, never accepting poor little Kyle even after he was born.

That memory twisted Shane's gut. He could not begin to imagine life without his son. Being forced into the role of a single parent had seemed unfair at first, but now he could see it was for the best. His widowed mother had finished raising him by herself with no ill effects. Therefore, he could do the same for Kyle, especially with a loving grandma as a mother figure. They were a tight, devoted family unit. They didn't need anybody else.

And he certainly didn't need to be looking for another wife. No way.

But if he ever changed his mind and chose to remarry, there were plenty of eligible, capable, single women in Serenity to choose from. So why did Jamie Lynn's image keep popping up?

There was no way he'd be able to get past Jamie's family connection to the loss of his beloved dad. Bringing excess baggage into a marriage was one thing. Having it include the matter of life and death was another.

He was not the kind of man who usually held a grudge, but in the case of Ray Jr. it was impossible to forgive.

He didn't care if he did admire her intelligence and courage. There was no way he'd ever let that woman into his heart.

Or into any facet of his personal life. Period.

EIGHT

Counting the minutes until it was time to leave for Marsha's, Jamie distracted herself by taking Ulysses to the city park for exercise. It hadn't changed a bit since her days in Serenity. The big lake in the center was home to geese and ducks, the asphalt walking trail had been kept up pretty well and the grass beneath the mature oak, hickory and pine trees was mowed short enough to discourage ticks and chiggers. All in all, it was a pleasant place to relax.

Children laughed and played on the swings and other equipment. Couples strolled hand in hand. Nostalgia threatened to overwhelm her.

Straining at the end of his leash, Ulysses distracted her by barking at nearby geese, and Jamie had to scoop him up to protect him from the defensive gander.

"You and I had better walk on the other side of the lake, dog, or we'll both get goose-nipped."

Because her pet was not easily convinced, she carried him halfway around the large body of water before setting him down again.

The sun was warm, the breezes gentle. A wooden-slatted bench invited rest and she accepted, closing her eyes and taking a deep, settling breath.

Why couldn't life be sweet and simple like this all the time? Why was she so fixated on making up for lost time and finding out what had really happened when R.J. had gotten into so much trouble?

"Because it's the right thing to do," she told herself. Would she feel that way if she hadn't begun this quest? Perhaps. Perhaps not. But she had stirred up the hornet's nest and it was too late to just walk away.

Glancing over the shimmering water and watching the graceful glide of ducks and geese, she let her gaze drift to the parking lot across the lake. Most of the vehicles that had been there when she'd arrived were gone and it was easy to pick out her truck, even though it was black.

Ulysses had been happily sniffing every weed and blade of grass near the bench. Jamie Lynn was smiling down at him when she noticed his posture change. He stiffened. Stared across the water. Growled for a moment before starting to bark as if defending her from a pride of charging lions.

That was when she heard the first crash. Saw movement. Understood why her little dog was upset and jumped to her feet. Somebody was bashing her truck with a sledgehammer!

"No! Stop!"

Shouting was futile. They were too far away and wouldn't have heeded her if she'd been standing next to them—except to perhaps turn the hammer on her!

"Thank God I'm not still over there," she whispered, realizing her words were heartfelt. She *did* thank God. There was no other plausible explanation for her ending up so far away when the trouble started. Ulysses's barking at the geese had been the trigger, yes, but the park covered many acres. What were the chances that the tiny flock would be close by when she'd arrived?

She had her cell with her. Punching in 911, she fidgeted, hoping help would come while she still had enough truck left to salvage.

"Sheriff's office. What's your emergency?"

"Somebody's beating on my truck!"

"Are you in the vehicle?"

"No."

"Are you in any danger, ma'am?"

"Not exactly, but…"

"All right. Give me your location and I'll send someone out."

"I'm at the Serenity Park. Please hurry." When the dispatcher spoke again, Jamie Lynn was positive she recognized her voice, not to mention her attitude.

"Ah, that's local police jurisdiction. You can stay on the line if you want while I see if they have any units available."

Jamie tamped down her anger long enough to learn that the estimated time of arrival of law enforcement was up to half an hour.

As soon as she hung up she let loose with a combination shout and growl that was so loud, so forceful, it startled Ulysses and echoed back to her.

Bystanders were starting to edge toward the parking lot, clearly cautious as well as curious.

The banging noise stopped. Moments later a truck sped away. Jamie Lynn scooped up her barking dog and headed back around the lake. Even if she had run, there was no way she'd have gotten there in time to see the license plate, assuming this truck had not been stolen like the other one at the old farm.

The closer she got, the worse the damaged metal looked. "Terrific. *Now* what?"

There was only one thing she could do. Like it or not, she had to wait and make another police report. Which meant she'd probably be delayed getting to Marsha's.

She punched in the woman's home number and started to fill her in as soon as she answered.

"No, no, I'm all right," Jamie insisted when Marsha interrupted to pepper her with questions. "I was all the way across the lake when it happened, Yes, I've called the sheriff. That dispatcher must hate me by now. She told me I'd have to wait for the local police. I'm stuck here until they arrive, and who knows how long that will really be."

"Stay put," Jamie heard Marsha say. There was garbled, muffled conversation in the background.

A few people had gotten up the courage to join Jamie and were trying to talk above Ulysses's barking, so she had trouble hearing everything that was being said on the phone. She covered her other ear with her hand. "What? I'm sorry, I didn't get that."

"Just keep your distance," Marsha shouted. "I'll call Harlan. I know he'll come out if I ask him."

At that point, Jamie didn't care who showed up. She just wanted to know that someone in authority was on her side. Cared what befell her. Wanted to help. At times like this it was easy to recall how abandoned and alone she'd felt when she'd first arrived at Tessie's.

Vulnerability was *not* a pleasant sensation.

Shane wheeled his rig into the parking lot before the arrival of any patrol cars. It was easy to guess where

Jamie Lynn was because a knot of people had gathered near a battered truck. Hers.

Evening shadows were lengthening but the air remained balmy as he climbed down and started toward her. Seeing her expression of relief and the way her eyes lit up when she spotted him in the milling crowd made his insides curl and twist. He couldn't help being glad to see she was unhurt.

She headed straight for him. "You didn't have to bother. The sheriff is supposed to be on his way. So are the city police."

"I know. Mom was phoning Harlan when I left." Out of things to say, he added the first thought that popped into his mind. "I just figured you might need a tow, so…"

"Right. I should have noticed what you were driving. Business as usual."

Shane wanted to take back the suggestion that he'd only shown up to make a few bucks, yet he didn't know how to mend the rift without sounding too personally concerned about her. Never mind that he was, in spite of his vows to the contrary. It was one thing to constantly think about Jamie Lynn and quite another to *admit* it, particularly to her.

Quickly, Jamie Lynn told him what had happened to her truck. Shane sighed. "I can stay here with you until the sheriff shows up if you want."

"I hate to ask it."

"You didn't. I offered."

"You did, didn't you?"

A smile lifted the corners of her mouth enough to make her dark eyes begin to twinkle, and Shane could hardly keep from breaking into a grin, himself. "Yes, I did."

"Then, yes, please stay. I don't like feeling alone in a crowd."

He nodded. "I'd never thought of it quite that way. I suppose that comes from being new in town."

"Yes." Her gaze lowered and she studied the ground between them as if it was the most interesting gravel she'd ever seen.

Rather than follow the train of thought his mind was suggesting and start to dwell on the lonely weeks following his wife's desertion, Shane mentally shook himself and took up another subject. "Let's go look over your truck. Maybe I can get a few answers from people I know."

"Okay." She visibly brightened. "It's a better idea than my standing here feeling sorry for myself. I'm sorry I snapped at you. I'm not usually so moody, honest I'm not."

"You have had a rough week so far." He fell into step beside her, careful to control the urge to take her arm or guide her in any other way. "I don't suppose you've changed your mind about staying?"

"You must be joking! The more they try to scare me off, the more I'm certain there's a good, strong reason to stick around and keep digging."

"I figured you'd say that."

"I suppose you think I should give up and turn tail like a scared pup." Her hands were on her hips and she'd wheeled to face him.

Shane shook his head and smiled at her. "Nope. On the contrary. If I were in your shoes I'd do exactly the same thing."

"You would?"

A softening in her expression tugged at his heart.

He knew what she was likely to ask next so he cut her off quickly. "Yes, but I'm not in your shoes. This isn't my fight, so don't expect me to keep bailing you out."

Jamie began by looking astonished, then glared at him. "I don't believe you! Have I ever asked for your help? Well, have I? Except for towing my truck and getting it back on the road, and that was strictly business, I have not asked for one single thing from you. Not one."

"How about rescuing Useless?"

"That was the sheriff's request. He said so. And as for all the other times, those were because someone else sent you. Your mother, for instance."

He figured the last thing she wanted to hear was how cute and funny he thought she was when she was mad, so he kept that opinion to himself. He did, however, smile. "I tracked you down at the old police station after you'd been shot at."

"Did I ask you to follow me?"

Chuckling softly, he shook his head. "No, can't say you did." He paused, then added, "You make it awfully hard for me to be a hero."

"Are you trying to be?"

"I don't know." He shrugged. "Maybe."

To his relief, the arrival of the sheriff's car interrupted their banter. Good thing, too, Shane reasoned. He'd become so engrossed with Jamie Lynn he'd almost forgotten himself and led her to realize he cared.

If that did eventually happen, he was ready with the excuse that he looked after the welfare of all his friends and acquaintances. It wouldn't hurt to include Jamie among those. After all, his mother liked her.

Yeah, Shane silently agreed. Unfortunately, his mother wasn't the only one.

* * *

Darkness was encroaching and everyone except Shane had gone before Jamie was free to start for Shane's garage. She wasn't pleased to have to leave her truck there again, but without working headlights she didn't dare drive it at night. Besides, one of the front fenders was bent in so far that if Shane hadn't straightened it a bit with a crowbar, it could have ruined another of her tires.

As soon as she'd parked inside the fenced work yard, Shane switched back to his personal pickup and locked the premises behind them. Jamie handed off Ulysses, tossed her purse in ahead of her and climbed into his other truck. "Okay. Let's go."

When the vehicle remained at idle, she frowned over at him. Both hands were resting on the wheel but he was making no move to proceed.

"Well?" she said, ruing the tinge of annoyance in her tone. "What are you waiting for?"

One eyebrow arched as he glanced at her. "Did you want something?"

"Aren't we going to your mother's house? I was invited tonight. I thought you knew."

A tilt of his head and slight shrug of his shoulders was the only reply.

"What's the matter with you?"

"Nothing. It appears that you need a ride. I'm just waiting for you to *ask* me for it."

"Oh, for…" She blew a noisy breath. "All right. Will you please give me a lift to Marsha and Otis's, Mr. Colton?"

The satisfied grin on his handsome face told the tale.

He was gloating. Not that she blamed him, considering the way she'd confronted him at the park.

"I'd be delighted, Miz Jamie Lynn," he drawled, clearly accenting his already evident Southern twang.

Not to be outdone, she did her best Scarlett O'Hara imitation and replied, "Why, ah declare, sir, you are the most gallant gentleman ah have ever met."

He chuckled, then laughed, then laughed louder.

Jamie joined him. Hilarity brought a wonderful, contagious release of tension, and tears were soon streaming down her cheeks while they both roared and guffawed and chortled.

Although Shane didn't appear to be producing tears as copiously as she was, he, too, was clearly over-whelmed, so much so that he had yet to start driving. She fished tissues out of her purse and offered one to him while she dried her eyes and giggled.

He wiped his cheeks with the back of his hand instead. "Where did that dose of Southern charm come from?"

"Beats me. Probably the movies. I'm still having trouble understanding everything people around here say to me. When I checked into the motel and asked the lady at the front desk if she could give me a quiet room, she said, 'I don't care to.' If she hadn't been smil-ing I would have been sure she was turning me down."

"Around here that means, I don't mind a bit."

"Swell. So besides rescuing I need a translator?"

"You'll catch on. It won't take long. There must be some understanding left from childhood."

"Bringing us back to my reason for being here," Jamie said, sobering without great effort. "Marsha said you'd found the old records she wanted. Will you be able to give her what she was expecting?"

"I think so," Shane said. He put the truck in gear and pulled out onto the street. "I want to clean up the boxes for her, so she doesn't have them in the house yet. She has allergies and the dust is liable to make her sick."

"I can help do that. You can just stack them in her garage and I'll vacuum them clean for her."

"We wouldn't want to put you to all that trouble."

It was his tone rather than the words that gave her pause. Could it be that he didn't want her to have a chance to poke around in his dad's old files until he'd had an opportunity to remove anything he didn't want her to see?

"Surely you can't be afraid of what I might find. After all, you said your father was very honest."

"Of course he was!"

"Well, then, what's the problem?"

Even in profile she could tell he'd gritted his teeth. "I'm trying to protect my mother, that's all."

"What makes you think she needs or wants protecting?"

Shane apparently had no pat answer for that question because none was forthcoming. The only change Jamie Lynn noticed was the way his fists clamped tightly on the steering wheel and his spine stiffened.

Once she had a chance to speak with Marsha and share opinions, she'd know more. Until then, she planned to bide her time and keep her mouth shut.

That concept made her smile. Separately, either task might be doable. Together, they were practically an impossible goal.

NINE

It didn't surprise Shane to see his mother hurry to embrace Jamie Lynn first. Hugging all the time was a Southern thing, especially among the women, although he'd seen plenty of men greet each other with the male equivalent: an eager handshake accompanied by a slap on the back. And grinning. Lots of grinning.

This time, however, Marsha was clearly concerned. "Are you sure you're all right?" she asked Jamie.

"I'm fine. My truck, not so much, but I'm okay."

"Shane took good care of you? And Harlan showed up?"

Jamie nodded. "Yes. Can I bring my dog inside again?"

"Of course. Kyle is waiting to play."

"I'll get him," Shane offered, "if the useless little ankle biter will let me."

The smile Jamie bestowed was tinged with cynicism. "You should be safe unless I give him the command to attack. Then, look out."

Shane rolled his eyes. "Right. He may think he's tough but I know better." *Kind of like his mistress.*

"Ha! Wait till you see him in action," Jamie Lynn countered.

Opening the truck door, Shane didn't have to say a word to get the little white mop of fur to come to him. He merely held out a hand and the dog responded immediately.

By the time he had scooped him into his arms, Ulysses was wiggling happily, stretching and licking under Shane's raised chin.

"Hey! That tickles."

His mother smiled and pointed. "I'm afraid it's too late to tell your dog to attack, unless he plans to lick my son into submission."

"Apparently." Jamie sighed audibly. "I'm really tired. Can we go inside?"

"Of course. How thoughtless of me." Marsha slipped a motherly arm around her shoulders. "You can tell me all about what happened at the park while I make gravy."

Following, Shane heard Jamie Lynn say, "There's not much to tell." He agreed. That was just as well considering how the latest attack might have turned out. If she had been in or near her truck when the hammer-wielding thug had shown up, there was no telling what might have occurred.

His heart skipped. Sped. Was that going to become her enemy's ultimate goal? How long would it be before somebody decided that the only way to stop her from probing into the past was to eliminate her for good?

Sentiment argued against anything so drastic. Logic kept insisting that it was possible, particularly if her suspicions happened to be even slightly correct. The portion of his father's notes that he'd already read had opened his eyes to an undercurrent of immorality that had shocked and saddened him.

Calm on the surface, like a lake on a lazy summer day, Serenity harbored plenty of trouble beneath its sparkling ripples of peace and plenty. Hints of graft and other corruption abounded, although lack of proof had kept Sam from pursuing or prosecuting most cases. The way Shane saw it, his duty was to keep Jamie Lynn from making so many waves that she drowned under them.

And, from the looks of things, he added, watching the women enter the house, his life was about to get far more complicated. Nobody had to spell it out. Marsha Colton Bryce was fixing to step right in the middle of Jamie Lynn's investigation and get herself into deep, deep water. It was going to be Shane's job to serve as her life jacket.

If he could have stopped her he would have, but he knew his mother too well. The more he argued against her involvement, the harder she'd fight to continue it.

Beyond praying for wisdom and the safety of his loved ones, there was only one thing he could do. He had to step back, observe closely and try his best to be ready to intervene when the next catastrophe hit.

It was one thing to claim total trust in God and quite another to exercise that trust 24/7, without fail. Shane wanted to be a perfect Christian, which, of course was impossible because his humanity kept insisting that worry was necessary.

"Lord, I believe. Help my unbelief," he muttered as he passed through the door. That was a scripture he rarely quoted and he was surprised it had come to mind.

Given the challenges of his life since meeting Jamie Lynn, however, it certainly was appropriate.

* * *

Each time she entered Marsha's house, Jamie felt more at home. And each time she left, more bereft. That was disturbing, to say the least. Her real home was with Tessie. The only thing tying her to Serenity was past trouble, so why did her mind keep insisting she could find peace and happiness here?

She shook off confusing feelings and concentrated on appearing amiable during dinner. That wasn't hard. Marsha mothered her, Otis was like the kindly grandfather she'd never known and Kyle reminded her of dreams she'd once cherished of having a son of her own.

And then there was the enigma that was Shane. How could she possibly hope to ferret out the truth when chaotic emotions interfered and confused her? It was evident that he didn't approve of her plans, and part of her was a people-pleaser. The sensible side of her personality, however, insisted there was nothing wrong with her original aims.

Belatedly, Jamie realized Shane was speaking to her. "Sorry. What were you saying?"

"I'd suggested we take the first box into the living room and relax while we look through it."

"That sounds wonderful." She glanced toward the hearth rug where a weary little boy and an equally worn-out dog had curled up together.

"Don't worry," Shane said. "Nothing much wakes Kyle when he's asleep."

"I can't say the same for Useless."

Marsha chuckled. "Which is it going to be, dear? Are you sticking with Ulysses or should we call him Useless?"

Eyeing Shane, Jamie made a face. "As long as I hang

around this family we may as well do it Shane's way. Besides, the dog doesn't care. They sound almost the same."

Shane's eager "All right" was accompanied by a smile.

Jamie figured he was happy because he'd scored a small victory. Fine. Let him think she'd begun to agree with his notions. Giving in about this was minor compared with being allowed to look at the former sheriff's old files and notes. What she needed to do, she reasoned, was keep careful track of what she had and hadn't read so she wouldn't miss anything important.

Turned out that that wasn't hard. Most of the journals were innocuous. Boring, actually. They covered the day-to-day operations of the sheriff's office, with a few notes about personnel problems and neighborhood squabbles. By the time she had finished scanning the third one, Jamie Lynn's eyelids were heavy and she had made very few notes.

She yawned and stretched, taking care to not jostle the nearby napping child and his canine pal. When Marsha offered coffee, she readily accepted. "Thanks. I'd love a cup."

"You won't sleep well if you drink more now," Shane warned.

His mother huffed. "It looks to me like she's about to drop off just sitting here. So am I. Be a dear and fetch us both a cup, will you? I made a fresh pot after supper."

Jamie was so aware of the man's every nuance she sensed a reluctance that barely showed. He glanced at his mother, then down at the box sitting by his chair, then up at her before nodding and getting to his feet. "Fine. How about you, Otis?"

"Forget him. He's been sawing logs for half an hour," Marsha quipped. "I'll take mine with cream and sugar, please."

Jamie opened her mouth to tell him how she wanted her coffee but he beat her to it.

"I've watched you. Same as Mom's, right?"

"Right."

As soon as Shane had walked away, Jamie Lynn set aside the small pad of paper she'd brought for taking notes, dropped to her knees on the carpet and reached into the open cardboard storage box. Shane had been doling out the contents as if he'd planned what to show them. She wanted to see what he'd held back.

The stack of manila-colored folders she was able to reach consisted of unmarked files. That was the first oddity. The second, she discovered when she resumed her seat, balanced the stack on her knees and began to read.

Although the notes seemed random at first, she quickly realized they were filled with familiar names. Names she had seen while going over the trial transcripts. There was not a smidgen of doubt. Sheriff Sam Colton had been secretly investigating the judge and prosecuting attorney who had sent her brother to prison.

It didn't take Shane long to return with three mugs of steaming coffee. One look at the expression on Jamie Lynn's face told him she'd been busy in his absence. Not only was there a pile of single folders on her lap, she was leaning closer to his mother to speak aside.

He cleared his throat. They both jumped as if the first jolts from a stun gun had touched them. Jamie's eyes were wide. Marsha was squinting at him. She gestured. "When were you planning to let us see these?"

"Never." Rather than chance spilling the hot coffee, he set it on an end table. "I don't know where you two started, but if you read all those files, start to finish, you'll see that Dad never proved anything. His hunches were pure supposition."

Jamie snapped her jaw closed. "Supposition? Since when do lawmen go around writing down guesses?" She waved some of the loose papers in his direction. "Do you know who these people are? Judge Randall presided over my brother's trial and Abernathy was the prosecutor!"

"I realize that." He lowered himself into the same chair he'd occupied before. "The thing is, their unproven misconduct has nothing to do with you or your family."

"Does that make it right?"

"Of course not." Restless and defensive, Shane rose again and began to pace, hands in his pockets. "The point is, there is absolutely no proof anybody negatively influenced Ray Junior's conviction."

Speaking firmly yet not raising her voice, Marsha said, "What about your father's accident, Shane?"

"What about it?"

"Has it ever occurred to you that he was lured to that deserted dirt road for a reason?"

When Jamie started to speak, Marsha silenced her with a raised hand. "I'm not talking about who may have run him down. Not yet. I'm asking if the so-called accident was really murder in disguise."

Shane shook his head. "Nothing like that was ever suggested before or during the trial."

"That doesn't mean it can't be true." She pressed

her lips into a thin line, her mind obviously made up. "What I want to do, what I want all of us to do, is sift through this information until we have some answers. Not the usual ones, real ones."

"You actually believe it was a setup?"

"Why not?" Jamie interjected. "Think about it. If you wanted a patsy, who better than an alcohol-abusing teenager with a bad reputation and reckless friends? I know R.J. wasn't alone that night because he never went out partying by himself. It was always with a group, mostly boys his age and maybe a few girls. There also had to be one person old enough to buy liquor or a kid who could steal it from a parent's stash, so why was the prosecution unable to find one single eyewitness?"

"The other kids were scared," Shane offered. "I know I would have been." Judging by the way her gaze immediately locked on his, he realized she'd come to another conclusion, one that was probably not favorable.

"That's right! You were nearly as old as my brother, weren't you? You can tell me who he hung out with and who I should talk to now."

"I didn't run in the same circles," Shane countered. "I was only fourteen when my dad died. Three years makes a big difference to teenagers. R.J. and his buddies probably didn't even notice me back then."

"Agreed. But as the younger kid you'd have paid attention to what high school seniors were doing. That's only natural. And with a father in law enforcement, I imagine it was tough to decide whether or not to tell on them for infractions like drinking or smoking weed."

"I did what I thought was right. Still do," Shane said flatly.

"Fine. In that case, you'll be interested in helping us dig up the truth," Jamie concluded.

He noted that the two women had joined hands above the files and were clearly demonstrating solidarity. Their minds were made up.

"Looks like I'm outnumbered," Shane said with a huff. "I guess you can count me in."

"That's not good enough," Jamie told him. "I'm not asking you to overlook my brother's possible guilt, but unless you're totally committed to uncovering the details surrounding Sheriff Sam's killing, you may as well forget it. Marsha and I will figure it out without you."

"Over my dead body."

"Poor choice of words," Jamie snapped. "I didn't come here to get myself hurt—or anybody else."

Leaning forward, elbows on his knees, Shane did his best to appear commanding and in charge without browbeating her. "But you may anyway. You do understand that, don't you? These encounters you've been having can turn ugly in a heartbeat. Your narrow escapes may have been nothing more than God's providential protection."

"You don't believe in luck?"

He clasped his fingers. "No. I don't. I've seen too many instances where it's clear that the Lord intervened."

"Then what about your father? And my brother?" She scooted to the edge of her chair and the files almost slid off her lap. "Or my mom and dad? Tessie said that Mom believed Dad had been killed and his body disposed of. What about her, and women like her, who are so afraid? Why hasn't God rescued all of them?"

"I don't know. I'm not all-knowing the way my God

is, but I do know I trust Him to do what's best for believers, at least in the long run. The problem is that our minds are finite. We can't look ahead and see why things happen the way they do. Half the time, we can't even look back after everything is resolved and tell much. That's where faith and trust come in."

Jamie pulled a face. "Yeah, sure. Even if I could learn to trust God again, the way you say you do, how do I know He'd step in and keep me safe?"

Sifting through memories, Shane recalled something she'd said when she'd had shards of glass glittering in her hair. "Remember dodging the bullet in front of the old police station?"

"Sure."

"Didn't you tell me you just happened to bend over at exactly the right time?"

"Only because of the dog. I didn't see any danger."

"That makes it even better," Shane insisted. "You might have reacted too slowly if the Lord had left you to your own devices, so he caused you to duck early."

She rolled her eyes. "You don't really believe that, do you?"

"Why not?" He shrugged as he sat back in his chair. "I happen to believe that I arrived just in time to rescue you from the house fire, and that it was no accident you were way across the park when somebody started beating on your truck. Dodging a bullet you didn't see coming isn't any more far-fetched than that."

"Oh, sure. Then what about the guy who grabbed me outside my motel room?"

"You had your feisty dog in your arms to bite him, and I was standing by. The only thing better would have been having a cop stationed right at your door."

He saw awareness alter her mood a moment before she said, "That's right. The drop of blood. Did the lab get any results?"

"Nothing they could match," Shane told her. "However, it gives us a base to build on if we're able to ID a suspect."

"Do you think we ever will?" Jamie asked soberly.

Shane hated to see her enthusiasm fading. "They'll do their best at the state lab. We can't do DNA testing on this whole town but I think there will come a time when we've narrowed our suspects enough to know who to ask for a sample."

Jamie reached for her pencil and pad of paper. "We have to start somewhere. Even if you can't remember the full names of my brother's friends, can you give me a few hints on where to begin? Who to ask?"

Better that than approaching the judge or attorneys, Shane reasoned. Although anybody could have been involved in fixing the trial, those two were now his prime suspects. Them, and the defense attorney, Max Williford, who had left town shortly after the trial.

Locating that missing man would be his first goal. With the internet providing information on just about everybody, it shouldn't prove difficult.

And when I find him, then what? Shane asked himself. He would cross that bridge of confusion when he came to it. Yes, he would help the women. But, no, he would not consider their safety secondary.

It was his fondest wish that Jamie Lynn would separate herself from his mother and son as often as possible. The times when they were together, he planned to be on scene, as well. And when they were apart, Harlan had promised covert protection. That was a perk Marsha had earned by virtue of being married to Sam. Shane's most fervent prayer was that she would never need it.

That none of them would.

TEN

Something had subtly shifted in Jamie Lynn's mind while she'd scanned Sam's files, and she wasn't at all pleased. Anger, self-reliance and determination had become overshadowed by a growing sense of uneasiness, bordering on mindless fear.

It was one thing to suspect that her brother had been railroaded into jail and quite another to see the names of his enemies on paper. So what if the sheriff's notes were mere speculation? They were enough to convince her. There had to be a connection. And now that she knew whose backgrounds to probe, she'd either have to act or pack up and go back to Tessie's.

Quitting was out of the question, of course. Beyond that, she hadn't the faintest idea how to proceed. A quick glance at Shane told her little about his feelings in the matter. Marsha, however, was clearly plotting.

"Tomorrow is Sunday," the older woman said, focusing on Jamie. "The best way for you to get a look at both the judge and attorney is to go to church with us."

"Church?"

Shane nodded. "Yes. Unfortunately, both men are members of the congregation at Serenity Chapel." He grimaced, and Jamie saw ire in his gaze. "When you've read all my dad's notes you'll see that others are, too."

"People he suspected?"

"Yes. I don't know why he didn't take his suspicions to our pastor, Logan Malloy. Logan was a detective before he became a clergyman."

"Perhaps he did," Marsha offered. "Pastor Malloy would keep that kind of thing to himself."

"Even after dad was killed? I wonder."

Sitting ramrod straight, Jamie Lynn folded her hands atop the files still resting on her lap. "All right. I'll go. But we need to prepare. How are you going to introduce me—as a Nolan or a Henderson?"

"It won't really matter," Shane replied. "Those you want to investigate probably already know who you really are. Otherwise, why would somebody keep trying to scare you off?"

"Good point." She clenched her fingers together more tightly, hoping to still their trembling and mask her inner turmoil. Was she up to facing the men who had framed her brother? Suppose she was wrong about them? About everything? What if others were behind the killing of the former sheriff?

A shiver shot up her spine and prickled the hairs at the nape of her neck as her thoughts took another turn. *What if R.J. was one of those others?*

Shane leaned closer and slipped the remaining folders off her lap, returning them to the storage box. "I think we've seen enough for one night."

Agreeing, Marsha reached to pat Jamie's clenched hands. "This has been a rough day for everybody. I say we meet for church tomorrow, then go out to eat the way we usually do and discuss things further."

That brought Jamie out of herself. "I don't know if I brought proper clothes."

"Nonsense, dear. As long as you're wearing the best you have, nobody will think poorly of you. We may have a few rotten apples in the barrel—every church does— but the rest of us are a friendly, accepting bunch. That's the way it's supposed to be. And, truth to tell, everybody sins. If we had to be perfect to go to church, there isn't a one of us who would qualify for membership."

"I'd never thought of it that way."

Shane chuckled. "Except maybe for me. I'm perfect." He adeptly ducked the playful swat his mother aimed his way.

"He was a little stinker when he was a boy," Marsha said. "But I will admit he's always had a strong sense of right and wrong. It just didn't keep him from choosing to get in trouble from time to time." She gazed fondly at her sleeping grandson. "Kyle's a chip off the old block."

"The brightest ones tend to be like that," Jamie said. "Plus, he's sure to try to take advantage of any adult who feels sorry for him not having a second parent. That's normal."

Smiling with melancholy, Marsha sighed and said, "I hope and pray he gets over it."

"I did," Jamie insisted. "All he needs is plenty of love and a stable home life."

Although the older woman was nodding as if in agreement, Shane had furrowed his brow and tilted his head. Jamie Lynn faced him. "You don't agree?"

"I'm not sure," he said, speaking softly. "If you were truly healed, would you still be looking for a way to rewrite your past?"

"That's not what I'm doing. Not at all. You know exactly why your wife left and probably where she went. My family was torn apart and my parents vanished." She gestured toward the others. "If your mom went missing, wouldn't you sacrifice anything to find her?"

"Of course I would."

"Then try to understand my position. I wasn't sure before, but I am now. Everything revolves around your father's death. I don't believe it was an accident and neither should you."

She reached for her paper and pencil, flipped to a fresh page and began to sketch a timeline. "Look at it this way. First, Sam is suspicious. He makes notes and starts investigating. He's killed. There are no witnesses in spite of the fact that my brother never partied alone. He was drunk out of his mind that night so I don't know how he could walk, let alone drive. Maybe he was in the car that hit the sheriff, maybe he wasn't."

"Go on."

"R.J. keeps insisting he's innocent until halfway through his trial when my father disappears. By this time, Mom has already sent me away. R.J. changes his plea, gets convicted, and right after that my mother runs, leaving no trace."

"You make a convincing case," Shane admitted, "but it all hinges on whether or not my dad's death was an accident."

"You've read his notes. What do you think?" She was holding her breath, hoping he'd see her logic.

Finally, Shane sighed and said, "I think you're right. I'm not ready to exonerate your brother yet but I do agree that my father was murdered. Now all we have to do is prove it."

Few viable ideas came to Jamie Lynn other than the

most frightening of all. If they couldn't prove who had plotted to kill Sam Colton, perhaps their next best option was to prove who was trying to hurt—or kill—her.

Kill? Yes, she concluded, shivering as the truth became clearer and clearer.

She'd been fooling herself by insisting that her enemies merely wanted to frighten her. They were serious. Deadly serious.

And the next time, they might not miss.

After the dire implications of their evening conversation, it didn't surprise Jamie Lynn that Shane not only volunteered to leave Kyle with Marsha while he drove her back to the motel, but he also offered to walk her to her door.

"Would you like me to check inside for you?"

"I hardly think that's necessary." She paused in the doorway of 6-B and flipped on the entry light. "Thank you."

He touched the brim of an imaginary hat. "Anytime. I'll be by to pick you up for church at about ten thirty."

"Okay. Good night."

With Useless in her arms, she sidled through the door and closed it with her hip. It was good to be back where peace and quiet reigned. Where she didn't have to think about evil every moment and could kick back and relax.

She slipped off her sandals, set the sleepy dog on the floor and smiled. "Nothing like playing with a kid to tire you out, huh, boy? Maybe, when we get home, I'll find you a puppy playmate to keep you in shape."

Padding across the carpet toward the bed, she was startled to hear a low growl. Useless was frozen in place, staring at the bathroom. Jamie fumbled in her purse for her cell phone.

The bathroom door was starting to move. She stared.

Through the gap between the door and the jamb she could see a sliver of the mirror over the sink. Only shadows were reflected but there was no doubt. They were shifting!

That tiny room stood between her and the only exit. Even if she called the police it would take them far too long to respond. She had only one option.

Taking the deepest breath she could while trembling like dry leaves caught in a tornado, she screamed.

The bathroom door was jerked open. A huge figure in a ski mask and black hoodie charged out. Crashed into her. Propelled her backward.

When they landed on the bed, all the air was knocked out of Jamie's lungs. She began to kick and punch her assailant.

Only one name came to mind. Gasping, she shouted, "Shane! Shane, help!" over and over.

If he had hurried back to his truck the way he usually did, Shane would not have heard anything from Jamie Lynn's motel room. However, as he started to turn away, he detected muffled sound. Was that a woman's scream or had one of the guests turned on a TV with the volume too high? Pausing, he held his breath to listen. Nothing. No more screaming.

Then there was a crash. A distinct cry. Somebody was calling his name as if the person's very life depended upon him.

"Jamie?" He began pounding on her door. "Jamie! Are you all right? Let me in."

He grasped the knob and jiggled it.

Locked. Of course. And if she had followed his warnings she'd also have engaged the other safety measures. These commercial doors were heavier than normal so his chances of breaking in were slim. Nevertheless, he had to try.

He stepped back and took a run at it, slamming his shoulder so hard he wondered if he'd dislocated it. The door shook in its frame but stood strong.

Another piercing scream echoed, this time tinged with pain as well as fear. Shane was frantic. He cast around for a weapon other than the concealed gun he carried. If he shot at the door, there was just as good a chance of wounding Jamie as there was of stopping whoever was attacking her.

The large potted plant caught his eye. Without a moment's hesitation he grabbed it, swung back and threw it at the window. Safety glass shattered, clearing the space in a heartbeat.

Shane dived through, parting the heavy drapery as he passed. He rolled once and landed in a crouch.

A dark-clad figure on the bed pushed off and stood to face him, hands fisted, body poised as if every muscle was preparing for an assault.

It came. Shane was ready. He dodged at the last instant and the attacker stumbled.

Now that he knew exactly what he was facing, he pulled his slim automatic out of its belt holster, chambered a round and ordered, "Freeze."

The burly man sprang for the door instead, jerked it open and escaped into the night. Shane chased him as far as the exit and stopped. Not having to shoot was fine with him but he would have loved to land a punch.

A weak moan snapped him out of battle mode. He automatically set the safety as he slipped the gun back into its holster and returned to Jamie Lynn.

She had managed to swing her legs over the side of the bed and sit up. Tears streaked her face. She was gasping out ragged sobs and trying to talk.

"Sh-Shane… Oh, Shane."

He took a step closer and held out his hand, wondering how he could best comfort her after such a frightening ordeal. Any worries he'd had about the possibility she wouldn't want to be touched were banished in the instant it took her to throw herself into his arms.

Instinct took over. He pulled her closer, one hand on her back, the other stroking her hair, and said, "It's okay. I've got you. You're safe. You're safe. He's gone."

Despite those assurances, Jamie continued to cling to him, even when a crowd began to gather outside the room.

The manager pushed through. "What happened?"

"She was attacked."

"He come in through the busted window?"

"No," Shane said, "that was me. Apparently, he was already in the room waiting for her."

"That's impossible."

Jamie's hold tightened, and he returned the hug to further comfort and support her. "It happened. I saw it."

"Well, I phoned the police so they'll be here shortly. What became of the guy?"

"He ran off," Shane told her.

"Good riddance to bad rubbish," the manager said. "You get a look at his face?"

"No."

That denial was true as far as it went. He had not

seen the attacker's features except for his eyes, and those were shaded by both the hood of the sweatshirt and the knitted mask he wore. However, that didn't mean he couldn't identify the person using other clues. Height, build, calloused hands, the odor of diesel fuel and an antisocial attitude all pointed to Roger, one of the Lamont brothers, although it could just as easily have been Dougie. It was handy knowing everyone in town.

Something in Shane's posture must have changed without his knowledge because Jamie Lynn eased her hold, leaned back and looked directly into his eyes.

"You know him, don't you?" she whispered.

He cupped the back of her head and gently urged her to lay it against his shoulder once again. "Hush."

"But…"

"Not now," he told her quietly. "We'll discuss this later."

He felt her slowly relaxing, trusting him, agreeing via body language to do things his way this time. That was a big breakthrough. It also meant that he had just vowed to become as caught up in her quest as his mother was.

If he had not been embracing Jamie in full view of the motel manager and half the guests, he might have pushed her away and insisted that he did not mean to become involved.

To his chagrin, he realized he might also have reacted the opposite way and kissed her. Of the two options, the latter seemed by far the most appealing. And just as dangerous, in its own way, as chasing criminals.

"No. Absolutely not. I am not going to stay with Marsha and Otis. Not tonight, not ever." Jamie Lynn had stopped shaking and, other than a doozy of a sinus headache brought on by too much weeping, she felt strong enough to cope with accepting another room at the same motel.

"You heard the police. Harlan said the same thing. You shouldn't stay anywhere alone."

"Well, I'm certainly not going to bring my problems to your mother."

Watching his expression shift and his cheeks warm, she almost laughed out loud when he said, "You can't stay with me. Not if you want to protect your reputation."

She smiled and huffed. "My reputation? You mean yours, don't you?" Waving her hands in front of her as if wiping away the comment, she added, "I would never consider putting Kyle in danger, either. He's a darling." *And his daddy's not so bad, either.*

"Then what do you propose to do?"

"I don't know. I suppose I could slug a cop, get myself arrested and spend the night in jail, but that would mean I couldn't keep Useless with me. By the way, he's the one who defended me before you got here. You should have heard him growling."

It startled her when Shane balled a fist and smacked it into the palm of his opposite hand. "That's it. That's our answer—or part of it."

"How so?"

"The bite mark. That's where we'll start. If one of the Lamont brothers has a sore hand from where Useless bit him, that should be enough to convince Harlan to haul them both in."

"When?" Jamie asked, hoping he was planning to see the sheriff immediately.

"How tired are you right now?" Shane asked.

"I was exhausted until all the excitement started. As long as my adrenaline lasts a while longer, I'll be wide-awake."

"Good."

He scooped up the dog and grabbed Jamie's hand. She gladly let him do both. The aftereffects of their shared embrace that evening were still so vivid she didn't think she'd ever forget them. Nor did she want to. There was no time in her entire life when she had felt so safe, so comforted, so certain that all was well in spite of outward manifestations of evil.

Being totally truthful with herself, she had to admit that Shane's being a Colton and a dedicated citizen of Serenity bothered her less than it once had. It was the person, the man, who impressed her. He was honest. Brave. Intelligent.

She blinked back tears as she climbed into his truck beside him. Most important of all, he was on her side.

She was truly not alone anymore.

ELEVEN

Heading out Highway 9, Shane telephoned the sheriff's home and convinced him to meet them at the station. They were sitting in Harlan's office, with Useless curled up on Jamie's lap, when he arrived. His hair was mussed, his shirt tucked in haphazardly and his chin showed stubble. Add to that his reddened, sleepy eyes and Shane was glad they had solid clues to present.

The heavyset lawman circled his desk and dropped into a groaning swivel chair. "All right. Let's have it. This better be good."

His scowl was impressive. If Shane hadn't known him all his life, he might have been intimidated. "I know who's been stalking Jamie Lynn."

"How'd you figure it out? The DNA on your blood sample didn't help."

"I'm convinced it'll match one of the Lamont brothers. Probably Roger."

Lacing his fingers together atop his desk, Harlan leaned forward. "What makes you think so?"

"Because I came face-to-face with the guy who broke into Jamie's motel room tonight and he reminded me enough of the Lamonts that I'd be willing to testify to it in court."

"Whoa!" Harlan was instantly on full alert. He straightened and pushed back in his chair. "There's been another attack? Why didn't you say so?"

Shane shrugged. "I figured you'd already know. Don't you listen to a scanner?"

"Usually. I was so beat when I got home we shut it off. Anything in my jurisdiction comes straight through to my pager, so I'm covered."

"This was another police matter," Jamie Lynn offered. "The motel is inside the city limits. That's probably why nobody notified you."

"Humph. We'll see about that in the future."

"The important thing is, I got a pretty good look at the man in her room," Shane went on. "He was big and husky and his jacket smelled like diesel fuel."

"That's hardly conclusive," the sheriff argued.

"No, but it should be enough for you to exercise your right to bring them in for questioning. If they think I've recognized them, they may be scared or foolish enough to admit what they've been up to."

Shane felt a light touch on his forearm and looked to Jamie.

"And who sent them," she added. "They have no reason I know of to target me. Their names weren't in the transcripts."

Harlan's eyes narrowed. He studied her, then Shane. "Transcripts? Will somebody please tell me what's going on here?"

"It's complicated," Shane said. "We'd rather not say just yet."

"Complicated?" Sheriff Allgood lurched to his feet, palms flat on the desktop, body arching forward. "Beating around the bush is for lawyers. I deal in facts. If you want me to haul in possible suspects, you'd better level with me. Otherwise, I'm going back to bed where I belong."

One quick glance at Jamie Lynn gave Shane the idea she wasn't ready for full disclosure. A barely perceptible shake of her head clinched it.

Setting his jaw, he eased out of his chair and reached for her hand. "I'm sorry we bothered you, Sheriff. Good night."

"Hold on, hold on. Not so fast. There's no hurry. How about if I drive out to the Lamont place in the morning and have a little talk with those boys?"

Shane felt Jamie squeeze his fingers, so he said, "Okay. That's better than nothing. Will you assign a guard on her motel room for the rest of the night?"

"Can't do it, son. Don't have the authority." He arched a bushy eyebrow. "Why don't *you* look out for her?"

"He is *not* going to stand outside my room all night long," Jamie said flatly. "And I don't intend to put his family in jeopardy by staying with them, either."

"That's a wise decision," the sheriff told them. "I've been hearing rumors about Kyle being exposed to unnecessary danger. Next thing you know, somebody might decide to get the courts involved."

"Nobody better try." Shane was adamant. "I'll make sure he stays with Mom until everything settles down. And in the meantime, Jamie and I will rent connecting rooms."

"I don't care what arrangements you make." Harlan yawned and stretched his arms over his head. "I need my beauty sleep."

As Shane's glance met Jamie Lynn's, he was confused by her unreadable expression. Was she afraid of him? Worried about being alone? Or was she relieved? He could almost believe the latter.

"What do *you* want me to do?" he asked her.

"That's totally up to you."

"That's not an answer."

"It's mine," she said flatly. "I refuse to ask you to babysit me while your son is neglected or his care questioned."

"Kyle is never neglected," Shane insisted. "He can sleep at my mother's for as long as need be. When they meet us at church in the morning, we can firm up long-range plans. He loves his memaw."

Watching the rapidly changing emotions reflected in her eyes, Shane added, "You can bolt the door between our rooms if it will make you feel more secure."

To his surprise—and relief—Jamie Lynn laughed. "A fat lot of good that would do me if I was attacked. You'd have to run outside and dive through my window again!" She chuckled. "That was quite an impressive rescue, by the way. Nicely done. Thanks."

Seeking to bolster her spirits as well as distract her from bestowing unwanted praise, he reverted to earlier teasing and used an overblown Southern accent. "It's not necessary to thank me, ma'am. We superheroes live for the chance to dive through broken glass and race into burning buildings. It's our callin'."

Sobering, she squeezed his hand again. "All joking aside, Shane, I do owe you my life. Probably more than once."

"It's okay," he answered in a normal voice.

"Still, I feel bad about your getting dragged into this. And your family, too. Especially Kyle. I would never knowingly put a child in danger. I love kids."

"I know," was all he said. Thoughts and memories, however, were so poignant his heart hammered. If only his ex-wife had been a little like Jamie Lynn.

That wish settled only long enough for another to sweep it away like waves washing over the prow of his fishing boat when the Spring River was at flood stage.

The one thing he wanted most was impossible.

Above all else, he wished Jamie Lynn wasn't part of the Henderson family. There was no way he'd ever manage to get past the knowledge that her brother had confessed to murdering his beloved dad. The image of Sam's broken body lying in a muddy ditch would forever bar any personal relationship with Jamie Lynn.

There was no way to erase the past and start over, no way to go back, no matter how fervently Shane wished there were. Even if she managed to turn up enough evidence to set aside her brother's initial conviction, R.J. had been involved in the crime somehow. Yes, he'd been intoxicated that night, but he'd known too many details of the crash to have been totally innocent.

As Shane saw the situation, his best option was to help Jamie dig up the truth, then hustle her out of town ASAP and hope that everything settled down after she was gone.

And in the meantime? In the meantime, he'd do whatever he had to, including seeing that no more harm came to her.

He fisted his cell phone, speed-dialed his mother to tell her what was going on, then drove toward Serenity's only motel. Harlan's suggestion of adjoining rooms had been logical. Shane just wasn't sure he wanted to put himself in a situation so rife with the potential for gossip.

In the end, his problem was solved by the unavailability of connecting suites and they had settled for separate accommodations next to the office.

He escorted Jamie Lynn the few feet to her room and paused beneath the bright lights. "Are you sure you have everything you need?"

She nodded. "Yes. Thanks."

"Okay. Here's your keycard. My room is right there." He pointed to the closest other door.

"Good night, then."

Shane circled her. "Open it so I can check."

"I hardly think that's necessary. This is a different room. Nobody can possibly know I'm here."

"Yeah, well…"

"Okay. You win. I'd rather have you look it over than stand out here all night arguing." She used the card. "Knock yourself out."

As soon as the green light blinked, Shane opened the door. The small room was not only pristine, the drapes didn't entirely block out the bright lights over the parking spaces.

"Looks fine," he said, returning after making a quick pass through. "I doubt anybody will try to break in when this area is so well lit." He gestured toward his own room. "If you get scared, just holler."

"Been there, done that," Jamie quipped, making a face. "Once is enough."

Shane had to agree. He smiled and bid her good-night, waiting until he heard the click of the dead bolt in addition to the regular lock.

What a difference a few days had made in his well-ordered, peaceful life, he reflected with mixed emotions. There were times when he felt as if this was a nightmare from which he'd soon awaken. Other times, his previous existence was the plodding dream and the crispness of this new reality seemed far more satisfactory.

That didn't make a lick of sense, he added, shaking his head with disgust as he entered his room.

To his surprise and chagrin, he found himself continuing to listen for Jamie Lynn's voice, to anticipate the ringing of the phone by his bed. Wishing for another chance to come to her rescue.

Vivid images of the last time he had done so refused to go away. He kept picturing what had happened after he'd grappled with her assailant. His pulse was pounding, then and now.

He'd reached out to her.

She'd stepped into his embrace.

And stayed—*almost* as long as he'd hoped she would.

Sunday morning arrived a lot more quickly than Jamie had hoped. Sleep had eluded her for hours after she and Shane had parted, and although she knew he was close by, she couldn't seem to relax.

Ulysses was more than ready for a walk. She threw on some casual clothing, eased the door open and peeked out, almost screeching when she saw someone loitering. Shane.

"You scared me. What are you doing out there?"

"Waiting for you." Shane checked his watch. "Want me to walk the dog while you get ready for church?"

"How much time do I have?"

"Over an hour until Sunday School," he said with a smile. "But you'll miss our free motel breakfast if you don't hurry."

"Have you eaten?"

"I had coffee. We can eat together as soon as you're presentable."

"Assuming I can meet church standards," Jamie Lynn said. "I told your mother. I didn't bring anything fancy."

Taking the leash from her, Shane continued to smile. "Do I look underdressed to you?"

Actually, he looked wonderful, she decided easily, masculine in pressed jeans and shiny Western boots, yet balanced for worship service by his crisply ironed long-sleeve dress shirt. "You'll do," Jamie said. "How about the white linen slacks and red top I wore to your mother's the first time?"

"I didn't notice. I'm sure it'll be fine."

As she stepped back to close the door, Jamie was grinning. "Didn't notice, huh? Then why are you blushing?"

"I'm not." Shane looked to the dog. "C'mon, Useless. Let's go find some nice green grass."

By the time Jamie finished brushing her ebony hair and adding a decorative clip to keep it neat, she'd lost the lightheartedness of teasing Shane.

She pivoted in front of the mirror for one last wardrobe check. She looked confident. Self-assured. Capable. That had been her goal, of course. Now all she had to do was figure out how to hide her tremulousness from everybody, including Shane and his family.

One glance at her spread fingers told her that wasn't going to be easy. This was the morning when she was to meet two of the men on her list of suspects: the judge and prosecuting attorney. Marsha was right about this being the best method of introduction. Jamie just wasn't looking forward to any form of subterfuge.

A knock on her door snapped her back to the present. "Who is it?"

"Me and a useless mutt," Shane called. "We're hungry."

"Coming."

Taking a deep breath and standing tall, Jamie Lynn stuck her key card in her purse, opened the door and joined Shane. "What can we do with Useless while we're in church? I want him to be safe."

"I've already arranged to leave him in the office with Sadie's granddaughter, Weezie."

"Who?"

Shane laughed. "Her name is Louise but everybody calls her Weezie."

He opened the lobby door and they were greeted by an exuberant teenager with a mouthful of silver braces. The girl dropped to her knees in front of Useless. "He's *adorable*."

"Apparently he likes you, too," Jamie Lynn said, watching her usually cautious dog leap into the teen's arms and begin to lick her face as if she were a long-lost friend.

Weezie was giggling. "Oh, I love him! This is going to be so much fun."

"You don't mind?" Jamie asked.

"Mind? No way. I am so going to spoil him while you're gone."

Satisfied, Jamie preceded Shane to the food display, chose her breakfast, then found a secluded little table in a corner of the room before Shane prodded her. "What are you thinking about?"

She sipped at her coffee. "My parents. I knew they were uptight about my brother's trial but I had no idea anybody had been threatened. When Mom sent me to Tessie's, I assumed the visit would be short. It wasn't."

"You never came home again?"

Jamie Lynn shook her head. "Not until now." She sighed. "I think if the adults in my life had told me the truth back then, I'd have been much happier. I grew up believing I'd basically been thrown away."

"Sad." He covered her closest hand with his for an instant.

"Very. And confusing."

"How did you reason it out?"

"By concluding that they had chosen my brother's welfare over mine, and when he had disappointed them they'd washed their hands of all their children."

"Even though you were totally innocent?"

"Yes." She met his gaze evenly, meaning to assure him that she had had no personal knowledge of her sibling's crimes.

"That doesn't make sense."

"Neither does sending me packing and acting as if I no longer existed. Try to see it from the viewpoint of a ten-year-old, Shane. My house had been a war zone ever since R.J. became a teen and started to get into trouble. Things eventually got so bad I used to hide in my room and put a pillow over my head to mute the shouting." She pressed her fingertips to her temples. "I get a headache just thinking about it."

"You didn't hear what was going on right before he was arrested? Not any of it?"

"The first I knew he was in real trouble was when my parents held strategy meetings at the supper table. I remember him denying any involvement in the hit-and-run, then finally admitting he didn't remember driving."

"Go on."

Sighing gently, she met his inquiring gaze. "There's not much more to tell. I suppose he may have recalled details as time went on, but he never acted guilty around me. Mostly, he seemed sorry and scared."

"I can understand that. The authorities said he'd killed a man in cold blood."

Jamie Lynn suppressed a shiver. Hearing Shane put it so bluntly seemed callous. She reached for his hand but he'd already pulled it away. "How can you be so detached? All I have to do is think about what happened that night and my stomach ties in knots."

"Dad taught me that the only way to get to the truth was to keep your personal thoughts and actions under strict control." He leaned back in his chair. "It's a matter of discipline. That's one of your failings. You get too caught up in proving your own hypothesis and don't let yourself see the big picture."

"Meaning, R.J. is as guilty as the judge said."

"Yes. And he's right where he belongs."

"Then why are you helping me?"

"Mostly for my mother," Shane told her. "I want to give her back the peace of mind she's lost."

He didn't have to claim Marsha was unhappy because of Jamie Lynn's return to Serenity. It was clearly implied. And he was right, as far as his reasoning went. She'd been over and over the transcripts of the trial and had also sent them to a friend who was studying law in Rhode Island. Everything seemed aboveboard. There were no unexplained irregularities, no indications that the prosecutor or Judge Randall had done anything illegal.

The key had to lie in her brother's change of plea, she reasoned. Which brought her full circle. Back to her parents' fear. And her father's disappearance.

Meeting Shane's gaze, Jamie Lynn reminded him of their morning plans. "Shouldn't we be going?"

"It's not far. We have time."

"Since R.J. still refuses to let me visit, there's one more person I'd like to look up while I'm here," she added, rising and picking up her trash. "Does his old defense attorney go to your church, too?"

"Max Williford? No. He used to. I haven't seen him around in ages."

"I tried to find him online. I couldn't find anything to indicate he's still practicing law. Don't you think that's odd?"

"Not particularly. He may have changed careers in midlife. Lots of folks do that."

"True." Pausing until he joined her, she watched his expression closely as she added, "But they don't usually drop off the face of the earth. Would you mind asking Harlan to look into it for me?"

"Sure." With a shrug and a casual gesture toward the exit, Shane eased her ahead.

Jamie wished he'd allowed her to walk next to him because she wanted to see how long it took for his concerned expression to fade. Of all the officials involved,

Max Williford was the one person besides her brother who was most likely to know what had happened to cause the change of plea halfway through the trial.

She desperately hoped they could locate him. The deep recesses of her mind added, *Alive.*

TWELVE

Unsettling feelings kept Shane on edge during the drive to Serenity Chapel. He had wondered how long it would be before Jamie Lynn decided to look up her brother's defense attorney, once she learned his name. The problem was, Shane had already searched. The middle-aged man seemed to have dropped of the face of the earth.

The same as Jamie's parents did, Shane thought. He supposed that was not an uncommon phenomenon in a crowded city environment. In a small town, however, it was rare that someone wasn't privy to inside information. Not much stayed private. All he had to do was ask a few loaded questions and an answer should be forthcoming. If his buddies couldn't tell him, surely a member of his mother's quilting or knitting group would have enough facts to put them on the right path.

Taking Jamie's arm when she slowed her pace, Shane guided her to the front entrance. The double doors swung open. A crew-cut greeter with a smile as wide as the Mississippi Delta handed Jamie a bulletin and pumped Shane's hand. "Welcome, welcome. Glad to have you with us."

"Thanks, Don. I'd like you to meet Jamie Lynn Henderson. She lived here a long time ago."

To Shane's relief and approval, the magnanimous greeter shook Jamie's hand as if she were the most important person present. That was one of the secrets of their close-knit church's success. Everybody was welcome and accepted. A twinge of guilt rocketed up Shane's spine, reminding him that he would do well to emulate the genuine openness of the elderly man.

"Have to come early to get a pew in the back," Don said with a wink. "You'd best get in there and grab a good spot for your guest."

"Mom promised to save us places."

"Wouldn't count on it. Not this morning. Marsha and Kyle headed for Children's Church when she found out they were shorthanded. I reckon she'll stay back there."

"Okay. Thanks."

"Does everybody keep track of everybody else around here?" Jamie Lynn asked aside.

Shane chuckled. "Lots of times it's handy. Like now."

As she slipped her hand through the crook of his elbow, she leaned closer to whisper, "I'm not sure I'd recognize Randall or Abernathy from the old newspaper photos of the trial. Do you see them yet?"

"No. They usually sit with their wives on the far side of the sanctuary, about halfway back." He gestured with a tilt of his head. "I never paid attention to what they drove or whether they came early or waited for the service at eleven. We'll go scope out the parking lot if I don't spot them pretty soon."

"Okay." Her grip tightened.

"Relax. Nothing bad is going to happen to you in church." He felt her shiver.

There was plenty of unoccupied space in the sanctuary. Shane chose to escort Jamie Lynn along the back aisle while he checked the congregation for the men they sought. Neither was present. Yet.

"Why don't I show you around?" Shane suggested. "Give you something to do besides sit here and fret."

"Sounds like a good plan."

"Speaking of plans, coming here to meet these guys was my mother's idea. She should be doing this with us."

"We could find her and ask her," Jamie suggested.

He was delighted to see her unwinding a bit as they left the main sanctuary and started down a hallway toward the fellowship hall and kitchen. The nursery, pastor's office and other Sunday school rooms were also clustered at the rear of the architecturally simple structure.

"We have expansion plans for back here," Shane explained. "That's why this part isn't bricked up fancy on the outside the way the front is. When we're done, the building will be shaped like a big cross and we'll have room to expand the core as needed."

Not receiving any comment, he paused and studied Jamie Lynn's face. She had paled and was staring out the windows at the paved parking area.

"What is it? What's wrong? Do you see the judge?"

"No, no, I was just remembering."

"Something about the case?"

"You could say that."

Frustrated, he pivoted and cupped her shoulders to look her straight in the eyes. "What? Tell me. It might be important."

"Only to me," she said. "Right outside our little country church—the one that used to be in Kittle—is where they arrested my brother. I suppose I should be thankful they didn't drag him out while the preaching was going on. I just wish they hadn't done it in front of our friends and neighbors."

"I'm sorry," he said, meaning it with all his heart. "Is that when you stopped attending Sunday services?"

"Pretty much. Aunt Tessie managed to drag me to her church a few times, but it was very formal. I didn't fit. Actually, I didn't fit anywhere."

Listening, Shane expected her to complete the statement by saying, *I still don't.* Although she did not voice it, the feeling was implied.

"You get along great with kids. Why don't you help Mom with the little ones this morning while I keep an eye out for our quarry? I can always come get you when and if I spot them."

Jamie Lynn's relief was almost tangible. "That's a wonderful idea—as long as you're watching to make sure I don't accidentally endanger the children by being around them."

"You won't. Even in a peaceful place like Serenity we have men assigned to watch the doors and hallways during the services. It's too bad it's necessary, but the pastor felt it was the wisest course. I'll also advise him of your presence so he can take more safety measures if he wants."

"I feel like a pariah."

You look more like a naive, innocent victim, Shane thought, censoring his response to, "Don't be silly."

As he gently cupped her elbow and urged her along, he realized that she was right. She was an outsider. A stranger. Someone who, considering her background, would be slow to trust or be trusted.

It would have been nice to convince himself that there were plenty of local folks who would take to Jamie Lynn and gladly help her find out more about her brother's sins during his teen years, but he knew better. Men who had grown up there and were now solid citizens were not likely to want to reveal their past mistakes. And the ones who were still lingering on the wrong side of the law were dangerous, especially since her probing might lead to their eventual arrests. Little wonder someone had already decided to scare her off.

"Right in here," Shane said, knocking on the frame of the glassed-in area of the nursery door. The moment his mother spotted Jamie Lynn, she broke into a wide grin and hurried to welcome her.

The door had barely closed behind the two women when Shane wheeled and started in search of the pastor.

Being the son of a legendary sheriff was not nearly enough to equip him for amateur detective work. Being Sam's widow wasn't enough to protect his mother, either, even though Harlan had vowed to look out for her. They needed professional help. They needed the sage advice of former detective Logan Malloy.

And they needed it yesterday.

"Of course you can help me," Marsha told Jamie Lynn, giving her arm a motherly pat. "Children are the future of the church. We value them highly."

"I love their innocence," Jamie said. "Truth to tell, I envy them such carefree lives."

Though she nodded, Marsha seemed to lose some of her earlier joy. "Not all of them. We have some parents who send their kids to us because they know we'll feed them if they're hungry and clothe them when they have that need. We're glad to do it, of course. It's just sad that it's necessary."

"Your son is a good father. I can't imagine any woman leaving—" she felt her cheeks warming "—a sweet child like Kyle."

"Shane and Roz were mismatched from the get-go. I tried to warn him but she had him fooled. Took him for the house he built for her and a brand-new car. I'm just thankful she didn't want to share custody of Kyle."

"I thought they lived on a farm." Jamie busied herself gathering and sorting scattered building blocks so she could listen to Marsha without appearing overly interested.

"That's the old Colton place. I gave it to Shane to take care of when I married Otis. Might as well. He'll inherit it anyway, someday."

"Not soon, I hope," Jamie said with a smile.

"Good Lord willin', I'll be around a while yet," the older woman said brightly. "Have you gotten any results from that internet search?"

Jamie's brow furrowed. "What internet search?"

"Oh, I'm sorry. I thought…"

Straightening, Jamie positioned herself directly in front of Marsha and stared into her eyes. "*What* search?"

"The one Shane mentioned," Marsha said, acting reluctant. "I thought you two would be doing that together, especially since he stayed with you in the motel last night."

"We were *not* together. I had my room and Shane had a separate one."

"Well, of course you did. I just meant, if one of you

was going to use the internet at the motel, it would make sense if you joined forces." She was fanning herself theatrically with her hands. "Mercy, is it hot in here?"

"Not as hot as it's going to be if I find out your son has been acting against me."

"Why would he do that?"

"To protect you. He's told me more than once that he's only involved in my problems for your sake. He sees himself as his father's replacement, your guardian."

Marsha sobered. "I know. He's very like his daddy in some ways. Men of Sam's generation tended to see women as needing coddling instead of as equals—or even their betters." A wistful look led to the beginnings of a grin. "Bless their hearts, they haven't got a clue what makes us tick. Never did."

"I'm surprised you haven't explained it to him."

That brought a giggle. "Oh, honey, don't think I haven't tried. Shane's heart's in the right place. He's just acting the way his daddy used to, convinced he has to be involved in everything I do to make sure it's done right."

"That doesn't drive you crazy?"

Marsha laughed. "Totally bonkers. But he's a good son and a good man, so I don't complain. And, now that I have Otis, it's not as noticeable. I can see my son starting to do it with you, though."

"Only because he thinks he had to save my life several times."

"Are you positive he's wrong?" Marsha was frowning and peering at Jamie. "Shane hasn't told me half of what I've learned from talking to Harlan. You may be in serious trouble, girl. If I were you, I'd be real careful."

"I'm not going to run away like my mother did," Jamie declared.

"Fair enough." Lowering her voice and checking to make sure there were no curious children close by, Marsha said, "Just see that you don't end up disappearing the way your own daddy did."

Jamie shivered. Pausing, she gathered her thoughts. "You sound as if you know what happened to him."

"No, but if my Sam had been leading the investigation he might have gotten some answers. All the town law ever said was that Ray Sr. was missing. Watching your poor mama struggling after that was like standing at a railroad crossing and waiting for a train wreck.

"I was so caught up in my own mourning during that time I probably missed a lot of the signs, but everybody agreed. Alice wasn't just grieving. She was terrified."

"How can you be so sure?"

"Because she never went out, never answered the door or her phone, let the farm go to ruin and eventually took off in the dead of night. Does that sound normal to you?"

Picturing the run-down condition of her former home, Jamie Lynn pressed her lips into a thin line and grew pensive. Finally, she said, "I doubt I'd recognize *normal* if I had a handbook with pictures and instructions. I grew up thinking right and wrong were easy to tell apart and happiness was what you felt when your mama made your favorite dessert or your daddy fixed a flat tire on your bicycle."

"A child's view." The older woman gave her an encouraging pat. "We all go through stages of growth, Jamie Lynn, and I don't mean getting taller. In I Corinthians 13, the apostle Paul said he used to think as a child, then put away childish things to press on toward the goal that had been set for him in Christ Jesus. Maybe it's time for you to consider looking into that."

"I *have* a goal," she insisted. "I intend to find the truth."

When Marsha reached for her hand and clasped it tenderly, Jamie was emotionally touched. Aunt Tessie was loving, but not at all demonstrative. Since arriving back in Serenity, Jamie figured she'd been hugged and patted and comforted more than during her whole fourteen years away. It was overwhelming.

When Marsha smiled and said, "As long as you're sure you have the right goal, the one the Lord wants you to pursue, He'll look after you," Jamie had no ready reply.

It had been a long time since she'd wondered if she was doing God's will, let alone was His child. She thought she once had been. And as she'd faced recent problems and dangers, she knew she'd instinctively reached out to the heavenly Father of her youthful beliefs. Was that enough?

She raised tear-filled eyes to Marsha. "How can I know?"

Instead of providing platitudes, the older woman clasped both her hands and began to pray aloud.

There were no fancy *thees* and *thous*, no complicated requests that sounded scripted, nor could Jamie have quoted her words if she'd had to. Yet the result was profound. The simple prayer began and ended with thanks and Marsha spoke to God as if she knew Him intimately. Trusted Him totally.

Tears rolled down Jamie's cheeks. Tons of burdens dropped from her shoulders.

By the time Marsha said "Amen" and reached for a box of tissues, mere moments of time had passed, while years of suffering had slid away like summer rain falling from the petals of a flower.

Jamie Lynn blinked and blotted her tears. "Wow. Thanks."

"Don't thank me, thank the good Lord. He's the one who gives us the opportunities to help each other." Marsha, too, was sniffling. "And He never gives up on His children, no matter what we do or how far away we wander."

"Even my brother?"

"Of course. The thing a lot of folks forget is that we can be forgiven and still have to bear the consequences of our mistakes here on earth. Your brother can be pardoned by God without getting out of prison. You do understand that, don't you?"

"Yes." But she didn't like it. Not one bit. If R.J. belonged in jail that was one thing. If he was innocent, however, there was no way she could simply stand back and let him finish out his sentence without trying to help. Research had told her that many convicts insisted they were innocent no matter how damning the evidence against them was. In her brother's case, there was only his testimony and the supposition that since he had been found alone, passed out cold in his bloody, dented car, he had to have been driving when it had hit the beloved sheriff.

Nowhere in the files about the case was there any mention of fingerprints or DNA testing—which hadn't been as common fourteen years ago, anyhow. Understandably, the entire community had been up in arms over the death. Whoever had been assigned to gather evidence probably did it as quickly as possible, particularly since they were convinced they already had the perpetrator in custody.

Looking around the cozy Sunday school room, Jamie noticed that Marsha and another older woman had three little girls busy coloring background for Noah's ark, while Kyle and a friend marched pairs of plastic animals up its loading ramp.

"Do you think they saved the car?" she asked Marsha.

"I have no idea. Why would they? What do you have in mind?"

"The pictures showed B-L-O-O-D on the front seats." She spelled to keep from alarming the children.

"So? It was a bad accident."

"Granted." Jamie cleared her throat. "Suppose some of it tested out as belonging to someone other than R.J.?"

"It still wouldn't show who'd been behind the wheel."

Jamie Lynn began to smile slightly while helping a little red-haired boy search through a tote for a lost zebra. "Maybe not. Aha!" She held up the missing animal figure, grinned and handed it to the child. "But it would prove that there were at least *two* people in that car."

Eyeing Marsha, she asked, "Would you… I mean do you mind…?"

"Asking Harlan to see about it? Not at all, dear."

If she hadn't been surrounded by demanding toddlers, Jamie would have delivered one of the Southern hugs she'd become so fond of in the past few days.

Was that really all the time that had passed? she wondered silently. At times, it seemed she'd just arrived and at others, such as now, she felt totally at home, as if she had never been sent away.

Although that realization was unsettling, it also provided a measure of comfort. The very place she had convinced herself to hate was becoming a refuge.

And the people? Jamie glanced at Marsha and Kyle. The people were mostly loving and accepting when she had anticipated an overall reaction similar to the one she was getting from whoever was stalking her.

Jamie Lynn shivered. Folded her arms across her chest. The mere thought of previous attacks was enough to give her chills. To prickle the hairs at the nape of her neck and raise goose bumps up and down her arms.

Logic insisted she was being foolish. Imagining things. Letting wild thoughts take control and skew reality. She was in a church, among friends, watching innocent children reenact familiar Bible stories. Fear was irrational.

Turn around.

No. There's nothing there.

Prove it. Turn around.

It was all Jamie could do to make herself look toward the glass-topped door to the hallway. There wouldn't be anybody there, she insisted, beginning to pivot.

A man's face was visible through the glass for mere moments before he ducked away.

She gasped. Wanted to scream. Knew she should race to the door and peek out to try to get a better look at him.

Instead, her feet remained rooted while her brain tried to convince her that she'd imagined the face.

She closed her eyes. The image grew clearer. It wasn't his overall appearance that frightened her. It was his eyes. The way he'd stared at her. The hatred she could feel all the way across the room. She didn't have to know who he was to sense malevolence. Shane had been wrong. No place was safe. Not even church.

THIRTEEN

"You *knew* what he suspected?" Shane was astounded. "Why didn't you do something?"

"Your father asked me to avoid getting involved," Pastor Malloy said. "After he passed away I spoke with the new sheriff and did a bit of my own investigating. Nothing concrete turned up."

"But you believed Dad?"

"As far as it went," Logan answered. He rested a hand of comfort on Shane's shoulder. "We can't go around accusing people of bribery and other crimes just because we suspect they may be guilty. That's why courts require witnesses and proof."

"Honest witnesses, you mean." Shane was adamant. "Let me tell you what's been going on since Jamie Lynn Henderson came back to Serenity and started asking about the accident that killed Dad."

The pastor checked his watch. "Sorry. Can it wait until after morning services?" He smiled wryly. "The congregation expects me to preach in a few minutes and they get real testy if the preacher doesn't show up."

"I guess so." Frustrated, Shane stepped back. "I need to see if a couple of people are here yet, anyway."

Logan Malloy's smile faded. "Don't do anything you'll be sorry for. Leave the dirty work to the professionals."

"If I was sure they'd done their jobs in the first place, I would." He raked his fingers through his hair. "The more I learn, the more questions I have and the less I believe justice was served."

"Then take your concerns to Harlan or the chief of police and let them look into it. They're both good, honest men. You can trust them."

Shane huffed. "Yeah. I trust most of the folks in Serenity. That's why what's been happening to Jamie Lynn is so confusing. Somebody in this town is trying to scare her off and I intend to find out who."

He could tell by the expression on his pastor's face that the man did not support his amateur efforts. That was not a problem. If Logan was worried about Jamie Lynn's welfare he might be more likely to offer useful advice, or even assistance in the field, although Shane knew enough about the pastor's busy schedule to doubt he'd have much spare time. Folks who thought the clergy worked only one day a week had never followed a pastor around, day by day. Poor Logan had once told him that the only vacation he hadn't been called back from was one where he and Becky and their kids had flown out of state.

Given the stresses of that job, Shane hated to lay more burdens on Pastor Malloy's shoulders if he didn't have to. Maybe the man was right. Maybe he and Jamie hadn't made the best use of Harlan's talents.

Shane knew he was still wishing Sam could have investigated his own death. If he had, how different might things be?

For one, perhaps the Henderson boy wouldn't have been charged at all, let alone convicted so easily. If that had happened, maybe the whole family would have remained in town and he'd have gotten to know Jamie under different circumstances. Shane couldn't imagine overlooking her the way he must have when she was a girl. She was striking. Her ebony hair shone like the wings of a blackbird in the sun. Her deep brown eyes sparkled with golden flecks. And when she focused them on him…

Shane shook off thoughts of Jamie and started to follow the pastor back to the sanctuary. A sense of foreboding stopped him. The urge to look in on the nursery and children's church was so strong he couldn't push it aside.

Wheeling, he started to walk, then jog. Few others were still in the hallways and the last choir member was closing the door of the passageway they used to reach their assigned places. At the far end of the hall, one of the ushers was locking the exterior doors so they could be opened only from the inside. There had been a time when Shane had thought such strict precautions unnecessary. Now he was glad the safety measures were in place.

He slowed, rounding on the nursery door, and opened it quickly. The children were so enthralled in the Bible story they ignored him.

Jamie Lynn, however, crossed the room in seconds and instead of greeting him politely, as he had expected, threw herself into his arms and clung to him the way Kyle did after awaking from a nightmare.

"What is it? What's happened?"

"I—I thought I saw a face."

"Where? When?"

"At the door. Just before you got here."

He held her away, yet kept a hand on her shoulder to steady her. "I didn't see anybody in the hall. What did he look like?"

"I don't really know. I mean, I only caught a glimpse. All I remember is the way he was glaring at me. If looks could kill…"

Shane slipped an arm around her shoulders. "All right. Mom has plenty of help now. Why don't you come with me and we'll see if we can spot the person you think you saw."

She stiffened. "What do you mean, *think*? I saw him. I know I did. I got this creepy feeling and when I turned around, there he was."

"You were anticipating seeing somebody?"

"Well, of course I was. Otherwise, why would my skin crawl and my nerves jump?"

That admission was less than reassuring. Jamie had been through plenty recently. He wouldn't blame her a bit if she started seeing menacing faces where there were none. That was perfectly natural. When your enemies had no recognizable faces, any aberration would suffice, even a reflection in the glass.

As he guided her toward the congregants, he pondered the best way to let her scan them. Standing up front with Logan was out of the question and it was too late to grab robes and infiltrate the choir. The narrow entrance hallway the singers used, however, was dark enough to hide in.

Shane eased Jamie Lynn ahead of him, explaining as they positioned themselves. "Stay in the shadows and nobody will notice you," he said. "I'll be right behind you. If you think you see him you can point him out to me."

He sensed her success by her body language before she began to whisper, and he had to strain to hear above the choral singing and accompaniment.

"There. Third row back, right off the center aisle." Jamie's grip on his hand was so tight it hurt. "In the suit."

Shane leaned over her shoulder. "Next to the woman with bright red hair?"

"Yes. That's him. I know it is!"

"You're positive?"

"Of course I am. I just caught a glimpse but I knew something was different about him. It's the suit and tie. It registered the minute I saw him again."

"All right." Shane sighed. The older man had lost weight and shed most of his thick, gray hair since the pictures from the trial. That meant it was unlikely Jamie was simply deluded by previous influences.

Drawing her deeper into the shadows and shepherding her all the way to the rear hallway before he spoke, he faced her and said, "That's Benjamin Abernathy. The prosecutor who sent your brother to prison."

Jamie Lynn was not surprised to learn that one of the people responsible for R.J.'s conviction was keeping an eye on her. She'd already surmised as much—and then some. If they could tie this man to the thugs who had been trailing and assaulting her, perhaps that would encourage the sheriff to pursue further clues. Anybody who was so determined to stop her had to be guilty of hiding something pertinent to her brother's case.

"I want to meet him. Look him in the eye," she said, ruing the telltale tremor in her voice.

"Why don't we start with some of your brother's former friends instead. If Abernathy reacts poorly to running into you and makes a fuss in public, we may have more trouble getting others to talk to us." Hesitating, he kept asking via his quizzical expression. "You know I'm right."

"Doesn't mean I have to like it." She made a face. "All right. When can we start?"

"One of them sings in the choir. They'll file out before the sermon and we can catch Steve when he takes off his robe."

"What's his last name?"

"Fenstermeyer, I think. I've always known him as Little Steve. His dad is Big Steve." Shane smiled slightly. "Neither one of them is little anymore."

"I suppose I may recognize him when I see him. I wasn't around my brother's friends much. Our parents knew Ray Jr. was trouble. As a ten-year-old I idolized him, of course. I'd have followed him to the moon if he'd let me."

"I'm glad you weren't in the wreck with him."

"That reminds me. When I was talking to your mother this morning, I remembered seeing pictures of the car. There was blood on the inside, too. I can't find any mention of testing being done on that evidence. I'm not even sure it was collected."

"It must have been. Dad had set up careful procedures for processing a crime scene."

"Except, at the time, they didn't consider it more than a drunk teenager behind the wheel," Jamie Lynn argued. "Suppose there was a conspiracy?"

"Or worse," Shane said. "What if one of your brother's so-called friends was driving and they'd planned to blame him all along? That would fit."

"Why R.J.? He never hurt anybody."

"Maybe not, but his mind was impaired, either by drugs or alcohol or both. He'd make the perfect scapegoat, particularly if some of his buddies were on the wrong side of the law."

Jamie Lynn rolled her eyes at him. "Some of them? Try all of them. I can't believe any of those guys ended up as good citizens."

"Don't be too quick to condemn them. Everybody deserves a second chance."

"That is *exactly* what I keep trying to tell you," she stated flatly. "And my brother is at the top of my list."

Little Steve was "the size of a log truck," according to colloquial descriptions. He was every bit as hefty as the Lamont brothers, but Shane didn't suspect him of being involved in any of the previous harassment. He was too normal and too smart.

They stood back while members of the choir hung up their robes and filed out of the room. Shane stepped forward to stop Steve before he had a chance to leave.

"Hey, Steve."

"Hey, yourself, Colton. What's up?"

"We just want a word with you. It won't take long."

"My wife and kids will miss me. Can't this wait?"

Shane was shaking his head. "Afraid not." He gestured. "This is Jamie Lynn Henderson. You used to hang with her brother, Ray."

"That's ancient history."

"Not anymore. What do you know about the accident?"

"What accident?" His words were directed at Shane but his gaze never left Jamie.

"Let's not waste time," Shane said firmly. "You know more about the hit-and-run than you admitted. It's time you came clean."

"Hey, I wasn't there, okay?" Backing away, he raised his hands in front of him as if warding off a threat.

"But you know what happened, don't you?" Shane paused to give the other man time to reason. "All we want to do is find out the truth. If Ray Jr. was driving, fine. If not, we'd like to know who was."

Little Steve led the way back into the empty choir room and closed the door behind them before he said, "Look. I have to live here. I have a business and a family. If I tell you anything, you have to promise you won't reveal where you heard it."

"If you weren't involved, then you have my promise," Shane said. "Somebody has been harassing Ms. Henderson ever since she got here. She's even been shot at. All I want right now is enough information to stop whoever is trying to scare her off."

Steve pressed his lips into a thin line. He clenched his fists. "It might be more than that," he said, speaking so quietly his words were raspy. "You don't know what you've gotten into."

"Tell us." Shane felt Jamie Lynn grasp his arm and inch closer.

"Back then, a few of the guys belonged to that private club we used to hear about in high school. You know the one. If your family wasn't rich you weren't welcome."

"Probably why they never asked me to join."

"Me, either," Steve said. "But once in a while they'd befriend outsiders if it suited them. That's how Ray and I ended up keeping company with the regulars sometimes."

"Go on."

"I was never in on any plans for real crime. You have to believe that. If I had been, I'd have tried to stop it." He swallowed hard. "At least I hope I would have. We were all dumb kids back then."

"Why did they involve my brother in the accident and not you?" Jamie asked.

"Maybe because I didn't like to drink as much as he did. At any rate, I knew something was up when the whole crowd ditched me and drove off, laughing. There was one other car besides Ray's. I didn't think anything of it until the next morning when I heard what had happened."

It took supreme effort for Shane to stifle his anger. "So, Ray could very easily have been driving? Is that what you're saying?"

"No, no." Steve eyed the closed door and further lowered his voice. "Ray was already too shot down. He had to be carried to his car. Somebody else drove it while Ray bounced around in the backseat."

"Names," Shane demanded.

Sweat had beaded on the other man's brow and his face was flushed. "I really don't..."

Jamie touched his forearm. "Shane promised to keep your secret but I didn't. Either you give us the names of the kids who were with my brother that night or I'll stand up in front of everybody in church this morning and shout what you just told us."

"Okay, okay. It was Alan, Bobbi-Sue and Marty.

Those are the only ones I remember leaving with Ray. Honest."

Shane was astounded. "Who drove Ray's car?"

"Um, Alan, I think."

"Be sure."

Heaving a sigh, Steve nodded. "It was Alan. Bobbi-Sue usually rode with him so Marty must have driven the other car. I didn't actually see them leave."

"Okay. Get out of here before somebody notices us. I'll take it from here."

As soon as the door closed, Shane pulled Jamie closer and just held her while he sorted out his thoughts. Clearly, she had been right to doubt her brother's guilt, and for more reasons than one.

"I guess I was too young to remember those people," she said, leaning back to look into his eyes.

"You will when I tell you more. Their full names are Bobbi-Sue Randall, Alan Abernathy—and Martin Williford."

Her jaw dropped. "That's impossible! How could the judge and both attorneys arrange to take part in R.J.'s trial?"

"It's a small town and there was an even tighter good-old-boy system in those days," Shane explained. "Given enough incentive, money and power, it probably wasn't hard to do. It took all three to see to it that their kids were never mentioned in court."

"But, but…the defense attorney, too? No wonder my poor brother gave up. He must have realized he couldn't possibly win."

"That, and the threats against your family that your aunt told you about," Shane reminded her. "Williford isn't the only name Harlan and I've been trying to track down with no success. We can't locate either of your parents."

"Assuming they're alive," Jamie added soberly. "I suppose my mother may be, but according to Tessie, Mom was convinced somebody had murdered my dad. They must have said so to scare her. And it worked."

"When this is over and justice is served, I'm sure the story will make the news. Maybe she'll see it and realize it's safe to come home." To his relief, Jamie began to smile wistfully.

"'From your lips to God's ears,' as Otis likes to say," she told him.

"Are you ready to brave the congregation or do you want to leave?"

"We can't go. Marsha will expect us to join her for Sunday dinner after the service," Jamie replied. "What about Otis? Doesn't he come to church?"

"Unfortunately, no," Shane said. "Mom would love it if he'd keep her company but he's a stubborn old mule. Says his faith is just fine without being hit over the head with it all the time."

"I wonder if he's right."

"No telling. Pastor Malloy says that's between each individual and God. We can't judge another person's heart."

Jamie pivoted and reached for the doorknob. "That's not entirely true. I have a pretty good idea there are at least three black-hearted parents and three of their offspring whose dirty secrets are about to resurface and give them plenty of grief. What I don't understand is why God let my brother rot in jail for so long."

"Neither do I." Shane held the sanctuary door for her as she passed through. "We may never know. All we can do is bring our information to the authorities and step back while they work."

He knew he should not have been surprised when she glared at him and countered, "No way, mister. I'll talk to the sheriff and whoever else will listen, but I'm not going to sit on my hands while my brother suffers. I don't care who gets mad or threatens me. R.J. needs a new trial and he needs it now." Leading the way to the sanctuary, she added, "I'll go all the way back to Rhode Island to find an honest defense attorney if I have to."

He would have asked her how she intended to pay for the lawyer's services and begged her to be more cautious if he'd thought it would help. Unfortunately, she was plunging full speed into more danger.

A touch on her arm slowed her while they were still alone in the hallway. "Wait. Think for a second, Jamie. Any judge who's powerful enough to arrange a trial and wrongful conviction plus hide the corruption my dad suspected years ago is a force to be reckoned with. If you let him know you're onto him, there's no telling what he may do."

"I have to help my brother."

"And we will, I promise. But let's start by having a talk with Pastor Malloy and seeing what he advises. He told me to leave things to the authorities when I brought up the subject this morning, but now that we know more, I think he'll feel differently."

Although her jaw muscles tightened and her eyes narrowed, she gave in. "Okay. For right now, I'll keep my mouth shut. But the second I think these rats may walk free, I'm going to do something about it."

"Fair enough." In view of her righteous anger, Shane figured he was doing well to have gotten any promise.

Now all he had to do was keep her from acting like the idiotic heroines in the movies and on TV who walked into dark rooms and didn't turn on the lights.

Unbridled emotions were funny things. They could make fools out of geniuses. And often did.

Jamie understood that having dinner in a restaurant after church was common practice. The only surprise came when Shane drove their little party out of Serenity. "Where are we going?"

Seated in the narrow half backseat with Kyle, Marsha said, "Otis likes DD's Diner in Gumption. He's going to meet us there."

"It's a retro fifties place," Shane added. "The food isn't fancy but it's always delicious."

Jamie Lynn sighed and began to relax. "Good. I've had just about all the pleasantries I can stand for one morning. It'll be good to get out of town and kick back."

She saw Shane smile as he glanced at her. "I'm glad you feel you can relax and be yourself with us."

The truth of that statement hit her squarely in the conscience. "I should have been totally honest in the first place," Jamie said. "I really am sorry."

"We didn't meet under the best of circumstances. It's understandable that you'd be cautious."

"Not cautious enough." She pressed her lips together in a thin line. "I'm still not sure whether it's smart to confront the people I think are crooks or if I should bide my time and try to gather more evidence against them."

"If you're asking me," Shane said flatly, "neither."

"Then I guess I'm not asking," she replied with a chuckle. "Look. There's Otis."

"And a parking place," Shane said. "Must be our day."

Jamie agreed. Except for the one incident with the face peering through the nursery door, which still rattled her when she thought about it, the morning had actually been pleasant.

She stepped out of the way so Shane could help his mother down from the backseat. Otis was there to take her other hand, and the look in his eyes was so loving, so sweet, it reminded her of the way her parents used to gaze at each other. She blew a sigh. *So, so long ago.*

The men stood aside for Marsha and Jamie to enter the café with Kyle, then followed closely. The place was crowded. Only one table was available.

Following Marsha and the little boy, Jamie scanned the old movie posters plastered all over the walls. Black-and-white checkerboard floor tiles were accented by red-topped tables and matching chairs.

As they jockeyed for seats at the table, Jamie was about to slide in when Shane grabbed her arm. "You sit over here."

"Okay." Although she didn't ask why, she did shoot him a questioning look.

The tilt of his head was barely noticeable. She turned slightly. Looked at the table next to theirs. And saw a man she might not have recognized if he had not been glaring at her.

It was Judge Robert Randall.

FOURTEEN

By shifting Jamie Lynn to the opposite side of the table with his mother and Kyle, Shane was able to place Otis and himself between Randall and the women. He would have been happier if he hadn't had to turn his back on the man to do so. Judging by the expression on Jamie's face, she knew exactly what he'd done and why.

His mother didn't look pleased, either. She arched a brow at her husband, then gave Shane the same treatment. He shrugged in reply, ignored her and spoke to his son. "Chicken strips or a burger, Kyle?"

"Cheeseburger!"

Jamie leaned closer. "You don't have to yell, honey. We can hear you fine."

"Cheeseburger," the boy repeated. "And a soda."

"Milk," Shane said, eyeing Jamie Lynn. "We don't want you to eat junk food."

A resonant voice behind him caught his attention. He didn't know who the judge was ostensibly speaking to, but his words were clearly meant for Shane's party.

"I say, people who endanger children should lose custody of them."

Freezing, straining to hear more, Shane held up a hand to quiet those at his table and focus their attention.

"I know, I know," the judge went on. "It's up to the courts to step in when parents insist on keeping company with troublemakers. I've seen it happen a lot, particularly with single parents who don't keep track of their kids while they're at work or out on dates."

Shane's hands were tight fists. He was clenching his jaw. The moment he made eye contact with Jamie Lynn and his mother, they both shook their heads.

Otis was the next to speak. "You know, I'm not that hungry after all. What say we pick up a pizza on the way home, instead?"

By the time Kyle started to whine about not getting his burger, Marsha was already on her feet, had him by the hand and was well on her way to the exit. Jamie Lynn hurried after her with Otis and Shane bringing up the rear.

As Shane passed through the door, he glanced back at the area they had just vacated. Most of the diners were busy eating and had ignored their abrupt departure.

One, however, was looking straight at them. And grinning. Randall had made his point and Shane was so angry he wanted to wipe that sarcastic smile off the judge's face with his fist.

And land myself in jail for assault, giving him even more reason to go after Kyle, he reasoned, realizing that that might be just what the man had intended.

Instead, they would get him the right way. The legal way. A way that would make Sheriff Sam Colton proud.

"I miss you, Dad," Shane murmured as he trailed the others to their vehicles. He knew what his father would have done. He'd seen it often enough as a child. Sam Colton had stood up for the underdog and the innocent. He was strong and faithful to his duty, yet could be tender when the situation called for sensitivity. And he never quit. Once he was committed to a cause he never wavered.

Which is exactly why he was killed.

Jamie had begged off and asked to be taken back to her motel Sunday afternoon rather than stay with the family for supper. She was wrung out, physically and emotionally. The less time she spent with the Coltons from now on, the better it would be, particularly for them. She knew that. She also longed for the comfort that came from being near Shane, from listening to his ideas, from leaning on his strength.

What surprised her the most was how *much* she missed him. It was one thing to rely upon someone. It was quite another to feel such a deep yearning that it caused her actual pain—pain that even cuddling her affectionate dog could not ease.

By the time Shane called to tell her about their upcoming appointment with the pastor the following week, she'd all but given up hope. Hearing his voice gave her mood such a boost it was scary, and by the time he showed up to get her, she had to fight an almost overwhelming urge to fling herself into his arms. Thankfully the judge's threats against Kyle and her own sense of impropriety were enough to stop her.

"Are you sure Logan Malloy can help us?" she asked as Shane ushered her into the church through a side door. "He's nothing like the kindly old minister from the church where I grew up."

"That's not a bad thing," Shane countered. "Logan

is intelligent and savvy as well as having a background in law enforcement."

"Okay. If you think he can help, I'm game. I just don't want to do anything that might jeopardize you or your son."

"Judge Randall was a fool to threaten us in front of witnesses," Shane said. "If anything, he did us a favor."

"That remains to be seen. Let's go get this over with before somebody sees us together."

The pastor welcomed them to his office and shut the door. Jamie was surprised at how knowledgeable and open he was as soon they had filled him in.

"Actually, I've been in touch with Williford recently," Logan said. "Max needed a favor and I obliged. I'll phone him if you'd like and see if he'll agree to meet with you."

"You'll *ask* him? What if he refuses?"

"I don't think he'll hesitate," the pastor countered. "Sadly, Marty is out of the picture now."

"What happened?"

"Let's just say his youthful mistakes caught up to him and he didn't survive the health consequences."

"I'm sorry." It surprised her to realize she meant it.

"It happens in the best of families," Logan said. "Even Christians can go astray. We're human, after all."

"How far away is Max?" Shane asked.

"An hour or so. He changed his name and occupation."

"What about his wife?"

"She left him after Marty got to the end of his rope. Max thinks she blamed him for the loss of their son, even though Marty was an adult by then. You won't have to worry about her trying to stop Max from talking to you."

"Okay. See if you can set it up," Shane said. "As soon as Harlan gets something he can match to the DNA of the blood samples from the motel, he expects to be able to arrest the Lamont brothers. If they reveal who hired them and it's who we think, he can go ahead and question Randall and Abernathy. Before he has something concrete to go on, he's afraid he'll spook them."

"Is there some place Marsha and Otis can go with Kyle?" Logan asked. "A short vacation, maybe?"

Jamie leaned forward, elbows on the conference table they were sharing. "I'd suggested that already, particularly since Shane's worried about Kyle being made a ward of the court."

The pastor looked astounded. "Why?"

"Because of me," Jamie said. "Randall made veiled threats when he knew we were listening. I've stayed away from Shane since then, for the sake of his son, but that may not be enough. I wasn't even sure we should keep this appointment. At least not together. But Shane insisted. He has a stubborn streak a mile wide."

Shane frowned at her. "Then go home to New England and let the pros handle the case from here on out."

"That is not going to happen."

"See?" He arched his eyebrows at their adviser. "What did I tell you? She's impossible."

"Yes, but if she had not come back here and stirred things up, we wouldn't know what really happened to Sam."

"There's still no real proof." Seeing Jamie stiffen in the chair beside him, Shane reached for her hand. "Let me put it this way. We know Ray Jr. wasn't driving the car that hit my dad because he was passed out. What we don't know is who was behind the wheel and whose blood might be on the car seat. All the evidence from years past is stored at the old sheriff's station. As soon as Harlan has a chance, he'll go back there and look for it."

"You think they gathered those samples at the scene?" Logan asked.

"We certainly hope so." Shane held tighter when Jamie Lynn tugged to free her hand. "We aren't going to give up until this is settled and the right person pays the price."

Nodding, she spoke quietly. "Do you think you could see if my brother will at least talk to you, Pastor Malloy? He refuses to see me and I thought maybe, if you asked, he'd agree."

"I'll be glad to try," Logan said, making a note on the pad of paper in front of him. "I take it he's in Little Rock?"

"Yes. That's one of the reasons I came this far instead of hiring somebody to investigate for me. I wanted to see my big brother." She raised a hand to discourage comment and added, "I'm not expecting him to be the teenager I remember. Aunt Tessie pointed that out more than once. I'd just like to talk to him, face-to-face. Maybe, after he finds out how much progress I've made in his case, he'll want to hear the details from me."

"Or be scared to death that you'll disappear the way your parents did," Logan offered. "But I will inquire and get back to you. Where are you staying while you're in town?"

"The Blue Jay Motel."

"I'd heard there was some trouble over there. Was that about you?"

Shane answered for her. "Yes. But there haven't been any more problems since I moved in, too." Grinning wryly, he added, "I have my own room and we're both in the very front where the lights are bright all night."

"Kyle's staying with your mother?"

"Yes. And I like your idea about her and Otis taking him away for a week or so."

"Assuming that's long enough." The pastor rose and offered his hand to shake Shane's as soon as Jamie pushed back her chair. "May I pray with you before you go?"

Shane wondered if she'd object. To his delight, she grasped both Logan's hand and his, completing a circle.

Further lifting his spirits and confirming the rightness of their visit, Pastor Malloy offered a simple prayer that was both touching and easy for laymen to comprehend, meaning it was sure to reach Jamie Lynn's heart.

He could not have asked for more from the detective-turned-pastor, except the phone calls he'd promised to make on their behalf. The sooner they spoke personally with the supposedly crooked defense attorney, the sooner they could move on to the next step and the closer they'd be to a final solution.

That would mean Jamie Lynn would leave, he realized with chagrin. But as long as she went away well and happy, that would have to suffice.

One more conclusion made him begin to smile in spite of knowing how badly he was going to miss her. His late father would have absolutely loved the intelligent, capable, loyal young woman and would have wasted no time telling her so.

That, Shane would do before she left town. As long as he took care to be certain she understood he was speaking on his dad's behalf rather than expressing a personal opinion, there should be no problem. At least not for Jamie Lynn.

He hoped against hope that he'd be able to carry it off without showing emotion because it was starting to occur to him that her departure was going to leave a void in his life as bottomless as the enormous sinkhole at Grand Gulf Park.

Fidgeting beside him, Jamie Lynn cast a sidelong glance at Shane as he drove. "Thanks for coming with me to talk to Williford tonight."

"You had doubts?" He arched an eyebrow.

"Not about you. I am surprised he was so quick to agree to talk to me. How much farther is it?"

"We're almost there."

Most of her questions had been asked and answered when Shane had spoken with Pastor Malloy again. It made sense for R.J.'s former defense attorney to offer to meet in a neutral place, since he was apparently frightened of being discovered. And, that being true, he probably knew who was behind the sheriff's untimely death.

Would that be too painful for Shane to hear? she wondered. Or might he feel relief? Either way, they would soon have their first real chance to learn the truth, and her insides were pitching as if she were clinging to the seat in a rowboat caught in a hurricane.

Approaching a wide, modern bridge, Shane began to slow his pickup. "Remember Lake Norfork? The entrance to the campground and day-use facilities is right across the bridge."

Jamie clasped her hands in her lap to still them. This meeting was an answer to her prayers, yet she dreaded hearing more about murder. Such things reminded her that no one was truly safe anywhere, not even lawmen, and where there was corruption in the system, justice was a mere fantasy. The concept was unsettling, particularly since her brother was experiencing it firsthand.

Sunset painted the sky a vivid orange, with rays of pink radiating to throw color and shadows over the empty picnic area. An arrow pointing to a boat ramp led them down a side road where a single, dark sedan waited.

Jamie leaned forward and pointed. "There. Parked behind those trees. See it?"

"Yes, barely. That must be him." Shane let his truck idle and held back.

"Go on." She was adamant.

"Let's take our time. If we rush him he may get spooked and drive off."

"Okay. Then let's show ourselves so he can see who we are." Without hesitation, she jerked open the passenger door and jumped to the ground. "Come on."

Shane killed the engine and joined her. "You are the most cantankerous, foolish…"

"Hush. And smile," Jamie warned, waving. "We want the man relaxed. Look friendly."

"I am friendly," Shane countered. "It's not his actions that bother me, it's yours."

"Nag, nag, nag." She knew her flippant attitude didn't fit such a serious situation but couldn't help herself. It was a matter of resorting to wry humor or collapsing into a useless heap of jangled nerves. She chose humor.

Shane slowly raised both hands to shoulder level, palms toward the partially hidden car. He elbowed her. "Show him we're not armed."

"Right. I didn't think of that."

They were about five yards away when the driver's door started to open. A black-clad figure emerged. "That's far enough. Identify yourselves."

"I'm Jamie Lynn Henderson," she called back. "If you're Max, I came to talk to you."

"Who's he?"

"Shane Colton." She edged closer to the parked car. "He had to drive me because somebody wrecked my truck."

"I'm not surprised," the man replied. "All right. You can come closer."

When they were face-to-face, Max eyed Shane. "You're Sam's son, right?"

"Yes."

"No wonder you're mixed up in this." His eyes kept darting from side to side, then over their shoulders as though he expected an attack at any moment.

"Before I tell you anything," Max went on, "you have to promise you won't reveal your source."

"How can we prove…?" Jamie fell silent when she saw the abject fear in the older man's expression. He'd obviously lost a lot of weight since the trial photos and had let his hair go gray, but there was no doubt he was the person she sought. Living this close to Serenity, she wondered how he'd managed to keep his identity secret—unless he'd lied and had actually moved much farther away. That would make more sense.

Shane spoke for both of them. "We promise."

"All right." The former attorney mopped his brow

with a wrinkled handkerchief and cleared his throat. "There were four kids involved in the hit-and-run. Three boys and a girl. One of the boys was my son, Martin."

"That's why you took my brother's case?"

"Yes. When I was first approached, I didn't know the whole story but I was coerced into representing the defense." He swallowed hard. "Turned out I was as much a fall guy as Ray was. So was Marty. They'd been brought along for the ride while Alan Abernathy did his father's dirty work."

"What about the girl?" Shane asked.

"Bobbi-Sue Randall? She and Alan were an item all through high school. Whatever he did, she helped. Actually, I suspect she egged the boys on more often than not. The way I understand it, she was behind the wheel of one car and Alan was driving the other because Ray and Marty were drunk. The kids had made a false report of a drug deal about to go down in order to lure Sheriff Colton away from town."

"So they were all together during the homicide?"

"Essentially, yes." Max twitched, turned toward the woods. "Did you hear something?"

"No," Jamie said, although she stifled a shiver. The sun had passed below the horizon and not only was there a chill in the air, the deep shadows had begun to seem alive, as if they willingly masked danger.

Shane agreed with her. "I kept checking behind me all the way from town. We weren't followed."

"Okay." The former attorney drew a shaky breath and began to speak again. "I loved my son and I thought…"

That was all he said. There was a bright white flash in the woods behind him, the crack and whine of a rifle bullet, and the shattering of the car window on the op-posite side.

A second shot came moments later.

Shane launched himself at Jamie, landing beside her on the leaf-strewn ground.

The blow knocked all the air from her lungs. Shock kept her wondering what had happened for several sec-onds before she caught a flicker of memory that was so horrifying, so ghastly, it further robbed her of aware-ness.

Max's eyes had widened momentarily, as if he'd been punched. His jaw had gaped. He'd staggered forward.

And then part of his forehead had vanished in a hid-eous red mist.

Shane levered a shoulder up just far enough to draw his weapon. One look at Jamie told him she was proba-bly unhurt, although there were drops of blood spattered on them both. Her eyes were glassy, her lips parted. Thankfully, she was breathing hard and strong.

"Are you hit?" he whispered.

She didn't respond.

He shook her shoulder with his free hand. "Jamie! Answer me. Are you shot?"

Did she shake her head or was he imagining things in the dimness? Anything was possible. Right now, he had more pressing problems.

The way Shane assessed their situation, they had few options. If the shooter thought Max had told them too much, they would be the next targets. If his goal had merely been to silence the source of inside information, they might be spared. There was no way to tell unless they tried to flee and were cut down before they could reach his truck.

The night was humid. Quiet except for the buzzing cadence of locusts and an occasional whip-poor-will call. Park lights came on automatically and cast a sickly yellow pall over everything, including the boat ramp access road.

Shane knew they couldn't break out in that direction. It was a dead end. He'd have to turn his truck around and go back the way they'd come if they hoped to escape, which might mean carrying Jamie unless he could snap her out of whatever emotional state was holding her mute and immobile.

Listening for approaching footfalls among the dried leaves, he heard nothing. That meant only that whoever was out there knew how to be silent, not that they weren't sneaking up on the lawyer's car to deliver a coup de grace.

He pulled out his cell phone and dialed 911. Doing so brought a response and promise of aid but no definite estimated time of arrival.

The closest town with a fire department was Henderson, meaning it shouldn't take too long for help to reach the area. Nevertheless, Shane kept eyeing his truck and listening. Not only was there no appreciable noise from the nearby overnight campground, he didn't hear sirens in the distance, either.

Finally, with no further signs of a shooter, he chanced getting to his feet and peering past the lawyer's car. The original shots had echoed in the rolling hills around the reservoir, confusing him about the direction they had come from. He did recall seeing a flash, however, and searched the distant dimness.

Nothing moved. Nobody shot at him.

"Maybe he left," Shane muttered.

That notion helped him decide what to do next. Crouching, he grabbed Jamie's arm and shook it vigorously. She stirred. Blinked rapidly, as if awaking from a nightmare, then tried to pull away.

"That's it. Come on, honey. Get it together."

He rechecked their getaway path. It seemed clear.

"What…what happened?" she murmured.

"You were in shock. Can you stand?"

"I think so."

With Shane's help, she managed to rise, although she swayed against him. "Keep your head down."

"Why? I…"

Her sharp intake of breath told him she was remembering and he saw her begin to stare at the color spattered and smeared on her hands and clothing.

Shane shouted, "Hey!" and gave her a quick shake to jar her. It worked. Her wide gaze met his, and she seemed to understand enough to listen to him when he ordered, "Run!"

Gun in one hand, her fingers grasped tightly in the other, he lunged forward. One pace. Two. Three. Almost there.

He jerked open the truck door and threw her inside, then circled the rear in a crouch and slid behind the wheel, keeping low.

The engine roared. Its tires throwing up rooster tails of dirt, the truck slewed 180 degrees and was engulfed in a cloud of powdery yellow dust.

Shane straightened the wheels. Floored the gas. His hands were welded to the steering wheel. He clenched his jaw so hard his teeth ached. Beads of sweat broke loose and traced his temples.

Jamie started to sit up.

He stopped her with a shout. "Keep your head down."

"Was Max…? Did he…?"

"Yeah," Shane shouted. "Max won't have to worry about being discovered from now on. He's dead."

The noises Jamie began to make sounded like a cross between sobs and gagging. He didn't blame her. If he'd let himself dwell on his last glimpse of the attorney's face he'd have lost his supper, too.

Crime scene photos were bad, but seeing a victim firsthand was far worse. No wonder his dad had always locked his desk whenever he'd brought those kinds of pictures and evidence home with him. The cruelty and evil Sam saw all around him must have been a terrible burden for any man to bear, particularly a gentle soul like his father.

Yes, a small portion of justice had been meted out tonight. That didn't make it right. Shane still believed in the judicial system. With the right men at the helm, the guilty would be punished. At least that was the way it was supposed to work.

He grimaced. Right now, he'd be satisfied with mere survival.

FIFTEEN

"**W**here are we going? What about poor Max?" Jamie was still sniffling but at least Shane had finally allowed her to sit up, brace herself against the tight curves of the mountain road and roll down the window to get some much-needed fresh air.

"To the closest fire station. I hope they're waiting for a police escort before they respond."

"What if they're...? Suppose they...? Oh, dear. They could get hurt!" She knew she was jabbering incomprehensibly. Judging by the way her head was spinning and her thoughts zigzagging all over the place, she figured she'd do well to complete a sentence, let alone a coherent one.

Flashing red and white beacons atop impressive trucks greeted them as Shane wheeled into a wide driveway.

A firefighter, wearing a dirty yellow turnout coat with reflective silver strips and carrying a walkie-talkie type radio, waved him away. "Clear the exit."

Shane leaned out his truck window. "We just came from the shooting at the campground. I can lead you in."

"No need. We've got it. If you're a witness you shouldn't have left."

"I didn't want to stick around and become another victim," Shane told him. "Are the police on scene?"

Jamie could hear a scratchy transmission coming over the radio. Most of the words sounded garbled. "What did he say? Are they there?"

The firefighter nodded. He seemed to be studying both Shane and her. "You follow my first responders. I'll be right behind you."

"Okay."

Glancing at Shane as he pulled out, Jamie Lynn frowned. "Did he sound funny to you all of a sudden?"

"Yeah. I wonder what else they found when they got to Max. I sure wish we'd had a tape recorder running while we were talking to him."

"He might not have said a word if we had," she countered. "At least we know who all was involved in the hit-and-run and which kids were innocent bystanders."

"We still don't know for sure who the homicide driver was."

"No, but we're making progress."

Shane huffed. "Oh, yeah. Great progress. We've managed to escalate the situation from warnings to murder. Harlan will be thrilled, particularly since we're out of his jurisdiction."

"You should call him."

"I already told him what we were up to tonight. There's no hurry about the rest. We can fill him in after we get home."

A shiver skittered up her spine and she felt queasy again. "You told him? I can't believe it."

"Why not? He'd have helped if he could."

"Did he say so?"

"No. I didn't speak directly to him. Just left a message I figured only he would understand."

"You said we were going to the lake?"

"No." Shane was scowling at her. "What's your point? I trust that man as much as I'd have trusted my own dad."

"Okay. Suppose you're right. Unless you plan to blame the preacher, you're going to have to come up with a leak somewhere. If we weren't followed, then somebody was lying in wait for us. And for poor Max. His murder was no hunting accident."

When Shane answered, "I know," she could tell how upset he was. That made two of them.

Police cars, green park service trucks and red fire vehicles had clogged the narrow roads at the murder scene, so Shane pulled over. "I don't suppose it would do me any good to tell you to stay here and wait for me."

"Nope. Not a chance."

"I figured. Okay. Stay close."

"I wish I'd brought Useless so I'd have company," Jamie said wryly.

"Yeah, well, unless he was the size of a police dog he wouldn't be much help."

"He warned me about prowlers before."

"And bit one. I know, I know. If he'd been big enough to take the guy down I'd give him a medal."

"You don't have to get sarcastic."

"Whoa. Hold up." His arm barred her way like a gate. "Look."

"At what? All I see is way too many cars and trucks."

"Exactly. So what's missing?" He waited impatiently until he heard her quick breath.

"Max's car. He couldn't possibly have driven it."

"No kidding. So who did?" He elbowed through the crowd with Jamie trailing. Not only was the attorney's vehicle missing, so was the man's body!

A gruff-sounding park ranger confronted Shane. "You the one who called this in?"

"Yes." He pointed. "The victim and his car were right over there when we left them."

"Why did you do that?"

Shane fully expected Jamie to say something like, "Well, duh," so he hurried to answer first. "We weren't sure Max was going to be the only one shot. Or killed. Believe me, he was dead."

"You a doctor?"

"No, but…" The officer cut him off with a snort of disgust.

Jamie stepped forward. "If that man managed to drive off with half his forehead missing, he should be in the book of world records." She displayed her hands and forearms. "Look at me. At both of us. Where do you think we got *this*?"

Crime scene bags were quickly produced and scrapings taken from their arms and soiled clothing. After that, Shane and Jamie were left in the backseat of a patrol car while a more thorough search was made.

"You okay?" Shane asked quietly.

"I've been better. What do you think they'll do with us? Are we under arrest?"

"I doubt it. Until they find a body, though, we may be kept in custody."

"What do you think happened? Why would anyone

bother to move Max? I mean, he's bound to be found eventually and we'll be proved right." She took a shaky breath. "Won't we?"

"Probably." Shane pulled out his phone. "And just in case we are locked up, I think I'd better notify Harlan before they confiscate this."

"When you get done with him, call your mother and make sure she promises to take Kyle far away ASAP."

"What about Useless? Do you want me to ask her to keep looking after him, too?" The gratitude in her dark eyes warmed his heart.

"Would you? Would she? I hadn't thought about keeping him out of trouble, too."

"Considering the way Kyle and that mutt took to each other, I imagine they'll both be delighted. And Mom's a sucker for whatever her grandson wants. They'll take good care of your dog."

To Shane's relief, she kept quiet while he made both calls. When he ended the last one and bid his mother goodbye, he noticed that Jamie was staring out the window and into the woods.

He touched her arm. "Do you see something?"

"No. No, I was just thinking."

"Uh-oh. Dangerous concept."

"Actually," she said pensively, "I was wondering if the shooter might have figured we'd only gone a short distance instead of taking to the highway. If that was so, your truck could have been blocking the road the same as all these vehicles are now."

"Meaning?"

"He could have taken Max's car to the boat ramp. Do we dare suggest it or will we look guilty?"

"I think it's a little late to worry about that," Shane

told her with a slight smile. He banged on the car window with his fists. "Hey! Hey out there! Open up. We have an idea."

Repeated efforts were necessary before anyone outside the patrol car paid attention, let them out and actually listened. Once they did, however, it was less than a quarter hour before cars were being jockeyed around to admit a wrecker with a crane.

"Nice rig," Shane remarked as it passed. "A bit old but serviceable. Wouldn't mind having one like it."

"You men and your toys," Jamie grumbled.

"Women keep useless dogs or cats. Men like rusty metal. It's genetic."

"I wouldn't know. My father wasn't very mechanically minded. He was great with crops and ranching, though."

"What about your mother? What were her interests?"

"The same as his, I guess. They worked together to make the farm pay, at least enough to scrape by. Neither one expected to get rich. It's the lifestyle that matters more than profits."

"Did she have hobbies?"

"You're trying to distract me, aren't you? Well, it's not working," Jamie said.

"Actually, I started out to do that. But I got to thinking. People may change their names and try to hide their past, but they still have the same talents and interests. They can't help it. Wherever your mother went, she's probably doing some of the same things she used to do, only in a different context."

"Milking cows and canning vegetables? I doubt it."

"How about cooking for a living? Or maybe working with animals, like in a shelter or at a vet's?"

"Without more clues than that we'd never locate her."

"No, and we don't even want to try until all the criminals involved in my dad's case are in jail. It's just something to think about."

A shout echoed. Then another. One of the firefighters jogged back up the road and motioned to them. "Hey, you two. Follow me. They want you for identification."

"I think I'll stand back and leave that to you," Jamie told Shane.

He slipped an arm around her shoulders and gave her a squeeze. "Feel free to close your eyes when we get there if you want. I'm not going *anywhere* without you."

Cuddling closer, she wrapped an arm around his waist and leaned in far enough to rest her head partially beneath his chin. "Mister, if you think I'm going to bellyache about that, you're crazier than you think I am."

"I may be the crazy one," he admitted. "We're going to ID a body and yet I almost feel like smiling."

"I know what you mean. So do I. I suspect it's because we're both so happy to be alive."

And together, Shane added silently. *I'm in real trouble here. When we're apart I feel as if half of me is missing. That cannot be a good sign. Not good at all.*

Apparently, Max Williford's car had not rolled far after being started down the boat ramp because Jamie Lynn saw no divers in wetsuits. Someone had hooked a chain to the rear bumper of the dark sedan and the tow truck was easing it out of the lake.

Water poured from every opening. Men with flashlights shined them through the open windows.

"We've got a body," one of them shouted.

Standing in Shane's embrace, Jamie pressed her

cheek to his shoulder and pivoted to face him. As long as no one insisted she look at the poor man again, she wasn't going to volunteer. She knew the image would give her nightmares for years to come.

What he had managed to tell them was helpful, although incomplete. The only detail still unknown was whether Abernathy's son, Alan, had been driving the murder car or if Judge Randall's daughter was the guilty party.

They were both in hot water, of course. And both had had motive and opportunity. Therefore, it boiled down to the difference between charges of premeditated murder or aiding and abetting. She was certain that neither the judge nor the prosecutor wanted the truth to come out. Therefore, either could have shot Max—or hired it done.

She had to loosen her hold on Shane to allow him to step up to the car and view the remains. All he did was nod. That was enough. When he returned to her she could tell he was deeply moved.

"Are you all right?" Jamie asked tenderly.

"No." His arm slipped around her shoulders again and she didn't back away. "I don't know how my dad stood it."

"It was different for him," she said. "He saw the sheriff's job as his calling, the same way I think of caring for young children and you take care of machinery. It's what we do."

"I suppose you're right."

Shivering from the atmosphere at the scene more than from the evening's chill, Jamie Lynn forced a smile. She could tell it wasn't convincing because of the way Shane received it. One eyebrow arched. He didn't mirror her false mood. Instead, he grimaced.

"Know what I think?" she asked.

"I'm afraid to guess."

"Ha-ha. All I was going to say is that I think it's time you called Marsha again and made sure she followed your instructions about Kyle."

"Now *that's* a good idea."

"I have my moments." When she smiled this time, Shane reciprocated.

"Yes, you do." Keying in his mother's preset number, he held the phone to his ear while still speaking to Jamie. "Do you want to talk to Mom about Useless, too? Give her more instructions?"

"That would be fine. Thanks." She watched his face as he listened to the cell phone. Obviously it was ringing on the other end. The problem was, Shane had not begun to converse with anybody and his countenance was darkening.

"There's no answer," he reported.

"Maybe she forgot it at home. Or they could be in the car and don't hear the ringtones. How long has it been since your last call?"

He checked his watch. "Less than an hour. It feels like ages."

"I know. Do you think they'd release us if Harlan vouched for us?"

"It's worth a try. And while I'm at it, I'll ask him to swing by my mom's place and check on them, too."

"Smart man." Jamie's genuine smile flashed briefly even though their surroundings continued to dampen her spirits. Despite all their problems and the ongoing danger, she was thrilled to have made progress.

She continued to wonder how the assassins had learned of their meeting with the defense attorney and why they, too, had not been targeted. Marsha would probably claim that God had protected them, and that was certainly a possibility. Yet Jamie felt a growing uneasiness she was unable to explain.

What was causing it? What should she do? Perhaps their forced inactivity was getting to her. Once they were allowed to head back to Serenity, that nervous sense should ease. At least she hoped so.

Observing Shane as he spoke with the Fulton County sheriff made her desperately want to pace. She repressed the urge. It wouldn't help him to see how anxious she was. If she had her way, they'd simply climb into his truck and leave, whether that made them appear guilty or not.

Shortly after he'd hung up from speaking to Harlan Allgood and pleading their case, one of the officers on scene approached. "We have your names and addresses. You two can go."

"Well, that was easy," Jamie Lynn remarked. "Hey! Wait for me."

She caught up to Shane at the truck and opened her own door just as he started the engine. If he had not paused to fasten his seat belt, she would have had trouble securing her own before he hit the accelerator and they sped away.

"Did Harlan say something that scared you?" The question had to be asked. She held her breath.

"No. He said he's going to go check Mom's house and the farm, too, in case they went there. He told me not to worry."

"But you are anyway?"

Shane nodded forcefully and glanced over at her. "Yes. Aren't you?"

This was not the time for evasion or making excuses. The most important person in her life, whether she liked it or not, was asking if she shared his thoughts and feelings. He deserved to hear the truth.

"Yes," she said. "I can't seem to shake a sense of disaster. I was scared all along, but this is different. It started right after they found the car in the lake and it keeps getting stronger. I don't have a clue where it's coming from. Or why."

The wider gaze he sent her way displayed more than mere concern. It reflected the unnamed fear she'd been unable to pinpoint and gave her goose bumps. Whatever he was thinking, it was affecting him to the core.

"I have the same bad vibes." Shane's hands were gripping the wheel so tightly his knuckles glowed white when they drove beneath streetlights.

"What should we do?"

"You keep phoning my mother's house while I concentrate on keeping this rig on the road," he ordered, tossing her his cell.

Jamie was relieved to have something helpful to do. *I'll get a hold of Marsha, she'll tell me everything is fine and I'll be able to put Shane's mind at ease.*

The phone began to ring. And ring. Finally it went to voice mail. Jamie covered it and spoke to Shane. "Should I leave a message?"

"No. She'll be able to tell it's us, but not where we're calling from."

"Why keep that from her?"

It seemed like an innocent enough question until

Shane replied, "If someone else has her phone, we don't want them to know what we're doing."

"If someone else has her phone? Why...?" The unspoken answer lay so heavy in the air inside the cab of the truck Jamie could barely breathe. She knew exactly what Shane was thinking and it was so dire, so impossible to fathom, that she could hardly wrap her mind around it. His imagination had come to the conclusion that his family had met with foul play.

"No!" She grabbed his forearm. "No. Harlan is on his way. Everything will be fine. You'll see."

Shane remained silent, his focus ahead. He clenched his jaw muscles as tightly as his hands.

Jamie redialed repeatedly, getting the same results. Finally she laid the phone in her lap. Tears gathered behind her lashes and she hoped her voice would be steady when she said, "I don't know what else to do."

Though he never took his eyes off the winding country road his headlights were sweeping, he did say, "Pray."

She wanted to ask him how to make God listen when she felt so inadequate; how to be certain her efforts were good enough. But that was foolish. Nobody could tell her that in a situation such as this or any other.

Instead, she put herself out there as best she could, called to her heavenly Father the way she remembered Pastor Malloy praying, and trusted the Lord Jesus the way she had as a child.

It was enough. It simply had to be.

SIXTEEN

By the time Shane reached his mother's house in town, the approach was lit by red and blue strobes.

Harlan stepped forward to meet him in the driveway. "Settle down, son. They're not here."

"They got away?"

"Can't say for sure." He mopped his sweaty brow with a hanky. "We're checking the house and grounds. I sent other units out at your place. There's nobody there, either."

"Then why doesn't Mom answer her cell?"

"Beats me. Could be we're gettin' all excited for nothing. Marsha's not a helpless granny." He smiled wryly. "I'd hate to get on her bad side."

"She's a good shot but she's no army ranger. If somebody got the drop on her she'd do whatever was necessary to protect Kyle and Otis."

A shout came from inside the house and a deputy bolted out the front door. "We found the old man. Somebody trussed him up and stuck him in a closet with a dog for company."

"Is he hurt?" Harlan called back.

"Mad as a wet hen," the officer replied. "Dog's not too happy, either. The little stinker tried to bite me."

As Shane started for the house, he looked back at his truck to check on Jamie Lynn. She was standing beside it, apparently still trying to reach his mother by phone. Considering the police presence, he was satisfied she was safe enough. He was only one person. He couldn't look after them all. It was his son who had to come first now. And his mother.

If anything bad happened to either of them, he'd never forgive himself—or the woman who had drawn him away from them at such a crucial time. Even if she had not actually asked for his help this time.

Jamie Lynn had barely ended her most recent attempt at phoning Marsha when the cell rang. *Marsha!* It had to be. *Praise the Lord!*

She grasped the instrument as if it were a lifeline, which it was. "Hello?"

"Jamie…"

"Oh, Marsha, you don't know how glad I am to hear from you. We've been so worried. Shane is frantic. He's…"

A deep, raspy voice barked, "Shut up."

Startled, Jamie stopped in midsentence.

"Just listen," the voice said. "Tell Colton I've got his brat and his mama."

Jamie Lynn had to lean against the truck to stay standing. Her grip on the cell phone was so slippery from perspiration she nearly fumbled it.

"Where? Why?"

"I want the old sheriff's notes. All of them."

"They don't say anything incriminating."

"Let me be the judge of that." He laughed as if enjoying a private joke. "Yeah. I'll be the judge. And the jury."

In the background, Jamie heard a woman shout, "Don't do it! He'll kill us all. He's crazy!"

"Shut up," he roared, and it was followed by the sound of a shot. All Jamie could think of was where that bullet had gone. Who it might have injured. The taste of gall on her tongue was bitter. The notion of another innocent person dying deadened her senses enough to provide the false bravado she needed so desperately.

"Knock it off. If you shoot your hostages you have nothing left to bargain with," she said, surprised by how intimidating she sounded. "Tell me where you are."

Another coarse laugh set the hair at the back of her neck prickling and gave her goose bumps on her arms.

"You, of all people, should know, since you almost burned to death out here," the man said. "Tell Colton to come alone and to make it snappy. I'm not going to wait all night."

"We're at Otis Bryce's right now," Jamie informed him. "The sheriff and police are running all over the place. There's no way I'll be able to tell Shane without everybody else finding out."

"Then give him this phone. I'll tell him myself."

"Okay. Don't hang up."

She pushed off the side of the parked truck, hoping and praying her trembling legs would support her. Not only was she steadier than she'd imagined she'd be, she was able to break into a jog.

Passing Harlan without slowing, she plunged through the front door and almost collided with Shane and his stepfather. Otis was being helped to walk and had Useless in his arms as if the two had bonded perfectly.

Breathless, yet functioning via the rush of adrenaline, Jamie thrust the phone at him. "Here. Take this."

"Who is it?"

"Don't ask questions. Just take it and listen."

The expression on Shane's face changed from wonder to anger to fright in a matter of moments. He nodded. "Yes. I understand."

During a brief pause, Jamie made her decision. When Shane continued with, "The old Henderson place. Yes. I know it," she was already backing away.

Fading into the crowd on the porch despite her dog's whining.

Edging down the steps.

Her brother's freedom was no longer her most important goal. A different kind of task awaited her, one that might cost her more than she'd bargained for. Still, she didn't doubt she was doing the right thing.

Jamie felt as if her feet were moving on their own while her heart preceded them. Marsha's car was blocked in by patrol cars. Some of those were idling and she could easily have taken one, but arriving at her former home in a black-and-white was too dangerous for the hostages.

No, she reasoned. She had to take a vehicle that the kidnapper would be expecting. Shane's personal pickup. That was also the only way she could be certain of beating him to the farm in time to trade herself for his family.

It was right. It was fair. It was her fault an innocent little boy was in danger and her job to see that no harm came to him. Even if she didn't manage to free Marsha, as well, at least she'd be able to give Shane's son back to him.

Sliding behind the wheel, Jamie Lynn had to strain to reach the pedals so she repositioned the seat. The key was in the ignition. She turned it, all the time keeping close watch on the bustle of activity nearer the house.

The headlights came on automatically and illuminated the scene even more. Shane was handing his cell phone to the sheriff. They both froze. Stared in her direction.

Time was up. It was now or never. She threw the truck into Reverse, gunned the engine and backed into the street.

Shane and several officers started running after her. They were going to be too late. They'd use their lights and sirens to try to overtake her but they'd fail.

She merely prayed and resigned herself as best she could to whatever fate awaited.

As she sped through the night, Jamie Lynn realized that up until now she had been operating on the premise she would do the same for any child. Now she knew better. This was a sacrifice she was making for people she loved, a special father and son. She'd started this. She needed to finish it.

Her only real regret was that she might never have a chance to tell them how she felt.

How very much she cared.

Several times, Jamie was afraid she was losing control of the truck. It was far bigger than the pickup she was used to driving and her haste had caused her to overshoot more than one bend in the road. Thankfully, the ultra alertness brought about by a surge of fight-or-flight brain chemicals was enough to control her body and keep the vehicle on the road despite excessive speed.

Wheeling in the long dirt driveway of her childhood

home, she saw the skeleton of the old house for the first time since the fire. Most of the left side downstairs seemed to have collapsed but the bedrooms on the right still stood, as did the base of the porch.

This was it. There was no turning back now. Whatever forces were in motion would have to be dealt with. She could do this. She must. The most important little boy in the world was counting on her.

She killed the engine, then quickly opened the truck door, purposely sitting in the cab under the dome light long enough to be identified. Since the kidnapper was expecting Shane and the late sheriff's papers, she needed him to see who she was rather than arbitrarily shoot anyone who was a stranger.

"Assuming I am," she muttered, raising her hands over her head as soon as she slid out of the pickup. The more she thought about the voice on the phone, the more she felt it matched that of the crooked judge. Adding his reference to being judge and jury, she was convinced this kidnapper would recognize her on sight.

"It's me. Jamie Lynn Henderson," she called toward the dark, forbidding structure.

The only illumination was what was reflected from the truck's headlights and a half-moon partially obscured by drifting clouds. Normally, the night didn't frighten her but this one was different. She'd seen one man die already.

Don't think about that, she ordered herself. *Think about things that will help. That will make you stronger.*

It wasn't necessary to cast about for the right incentive. It came to her complete and ran through her mind as if she'd practiced it.

"'The Lord is my shepherd, I shall not want...'"

Jamie placed one foot on the bottom step, then the next. "'He makes me to lie down in green pastures…'"

She crossed the porch. Approached the open door. Passed through. "'He leads me beside still waters…'"

"Stop right there!" The gruff order echoed through what was left of the old house and raised the hackles on the back of her neck.

All doubt vanished. It was Randall, all right. And he sounded as if Marsha's assessment of his mental state had been correct. His devious mind had become unbalanced, making him far more dangerous than a rational man would be.

"I came to negotiate," Jamie Lynn shouted up the staircase.

Some might have called the resulting noise laughter. To her, it sounded like the evil cackling of the three hags in her college drama club's performance of Shakespeare's *Macbeth*. There was no humor in it.

"'He restores my soul…'" She took two more paces, pausing at the foot of the familiar staircase.

"I should shoot you where you stand," the madman yelled.

A dark shape loomed on the landing above her. "If you do, you'll be sorry. Don't you want to know what I've discovered? It's very interesting."

"Where are Colton's papers? Why didn't you bring them?"

"Because I don't have them," Jamie Lynn replied.

"Then what good are you to me?"

That was an excellent question, proving that the judge retained a portion of his capacity to reason, even if he was acting irrationally.

"Shane and I are…" She hesitated to lie, yet how far

from the truth would it be if she referred to a romantic relationship? For her part, there certainly was one. What Shane did or didn't feel had never been discussed.

"We're in love," Jamie announced. "If you take me, he's sure to listen and give you whatever you want."

"I don't need you. I've got his kid."

Jamie's heart leaped, her pulse pounding. "And his mother?"

"Yeah. Her, too."

In the ensuing silence she was certain Randall and everyone else could hear her heartbeats. She certainly could. They echoed in her ears and drummed in her temples.

Finally, the captor called, "Okay, come on upstairs. But no tricks. I'll shoot the hostages if you try anything."

Climbing slowly, her hands raised, Jamie heard the wooden steps creaking under her weight. They had been noisy for as long as she could remember, yet had never felt quite this spongy. Perhaps the fire had undermined them.

The shadow gave way as she closed the distance. He was close enough for her to attack and perhaps push over the railing, but where was Kyle? What about Marsha? There was no reason to risk her life until she could see them and decide what course of action would be best, yet the urge to leap at him was strong.

Randall cackled. "I can see you plotting, lady. It's in your eyes, in the way you move."

"You can't see my eyes. It's too dark."

"Oh?" The beam of a flashlight directed into her face was so bright it took several long seconds for Jamie's pupils to adjust. When they did, she knew what the kidnapper meant. He was not only armed with a pistol, he was wearing something on his head that looked like pictures she'd seen of night vision goggles.

She swiped away the tears the light had caused. "How do I know you really have Marsha and Kyle?"

"Because you talked to her on the phone, you idiot." The more Randall interacted with her, the more deranged he sounded and the more frightened Jamie Lynn became. Her strongest hope was that she was managing to mask her fear. Since he had accused her of plotting against him, perhaps she was succeeding.

"We're over here," a woman's voice called.

"Are you okay?"

"So far. What are you doing here?"

"I snuck away from Shane so I could be with you."

Marsha's voice wavered as she said, "What did you hope to accomplish?"

"I came to trade myself for you and Kyle."

Jamie felt the barrel of a gun against her spine and was shoved so hard she stumbled forward. The door slammed behind her, leaving only the faint glow of moonlight. That was enough to make out her fellow captives huddled in the corner farthest from the door. Marsha had shoved Kyle behind her.

"This used to be my room when I was little," Jamie said, approaching them and lowering her voice. "Are you tied up?"

Marsha shook her head. "No. I'm not sure he intended to take us. He was acting very strange when he came to the house looking for Shane."

"Tonight? He thought Shane was at home tonight?"

"I guess so. Why?"

"Because if he'd been behind Max Williford's murder he'd have known where Shane and I were."

"Not necessarily," the older woman argued. "He was rambling when he showed up."

"If he wanted Sam's old notes, why didn't you give some to him?"

"Because Harlan took most of the boxes. The rest, you and Shane had at the motel."

Jamie Lynn nodded. "Okay. I know I was followed from your house but I don't know how long it will be before help arrives. Shane is on foot because I stole his truck. If he wants to bring Sam's notes for a ransom, he and the sheriff will have to go collect them."

She eyed the window she'd had so much trouble opening. It was cracked, probably from the heat of the fire, and so smoky it was partly opaque. Hiding on the porch roof was no smarter for Marsha and Kyle than it had been for her when the Lamont brothers had been after her, but that didn't mean Randall would reason it out.

Jamie said, "I have an idea."

"No. We're fine for now. As soon as Shane gets here with Sam's files, the judge will let us go."

"In your dreams," Jamie countered. "Think, Marsha. What would your Sheriff Sam tell you to do? The judge has gone 'round the bend, as my dad used to say. This bunch of low-life crooks has killed Sam and Max Williford and probably at least one of my parents. What makes you think anybody is going to walk away from this mess?"

"We have to get Kyle out."

"Exactly why I came," Jamie Lynn said. Because the child was cowering behind his grandmother, she leaned past Marsha to speak to him. "I'm going to count on you to rescue your memaw. Understand?"

The tousled head nodded.

"Okay. Give me your jacket and listen, both of you. Here's what we're going to do."

SEVENTEEN

Anger took over Shane's usually logical mind. He shouted. Paced. Confronted the sheriff and was ready to take on every other uniform in sight.

Harlan startled him when he came up behind Shane and clamped a hand on his shoulder. "Whoa."

Whirling, Shane drew back his fist, barely able to control himself. When the older man ducked and looked concerned, it helped snap him out of his mindless rage.

He froze, still ready for a physical altercation, then slowly lowered his arm. His breathing was ragged, his pulse so rapid he could barely tell the beats apart. Every nerve in his body was firing and the connections in his brain were as snarled and tangled as the silk of a damaged spiderweb. He wasn't sure what he wanted to do next.

"We know where Jamie's going, right?"

Shane could only nod.

"Then let's let the police chase after her while we go get the stuff the kidnapper wants."

"It won't be enough. You should have heard his voice. He's lost his mind. There's no way we can trust him."

"That doesn't matter right now. Get in my car. We'll

swing by my office and pick up a few boxes to satisfy the judge's demands, just in case."

Moving as if his body were detached from his mind and he was merely an outside observer, Shane complied. Life as he'd known it was hanging by a frayed thread and all the events he'd once thought catastrophic paled in comparison. When he'd seen Jamie Lynn drive away, he hadn't been able to decide whether to shout or tear his hair out by the roots. Now he was so numb he hardly felt a thing.

He gripped the seat as the sheriff's car slued around another corner and bounced in and out of potholes on the dirt road.

"I should have known the minute that girl showed up that she'd be trouble," Harlan said. "Never did cotton to that family. Nothin' but a nuisance. All of 'em. Alice drove me crazy with her tall tales of Ray bein' buried."

Shane stared over at him. "Buried? I thought everybody said he'd run off."

"Everybody but Alice. She swore he'd ended up at the end of Creek Hollow, where the road peters out."

"Did you ever look?"

"I drove out there a time or two. There was no sign of a grave or any diggin'. Pretty soon, Alice was gone, too. Everything settled down after that."

"You never looked at any of my dad's papers? His private files?"

"Why should I? Anything that pertained to the office was right where it belonged. I had a couple of deputies gather up your daddy's stuff and take it out to Marsha's."

Where it sat in my barn gathering dust, Shane thought, *until a special woman set aside her fears and came after the truth.*

"What are we going to do when we get to the Henderson place?" Shane asked.

"Beats the you-know-what out of me," Harlan replied. "I notified the state and asked for hostage negotiators but we're three hours from Little Rock—unless they take a chopper and fly. I suppose they could do that, although I doubt it."

Shane wasn't going to hold out hope that anyone would arrive in time to save his family. If he let himself get angry again he'd want to storm the house, which was pretty much guaranteed to get him killed.

If Jamie Lynn had only waited, had let him come with her, maybe she'd have had some idea of how to sneak up on the judge. After all, it had been her home once and she'd managed to outwit the arsonists.

Stubborn. Pigheaded. Foolish. He ran out of derogatory terms and switched to complimentary ones. *Loving, caring, beautiful, intelligent, courageous* and right back to *stubborn.*

She was a contradiction in more ways than one. Her difficult life had matured her yet had also left her feeling alone and unloved. He wondered if time would have eventually healed her if she hadn't come back to Serenity. Perhaps. Perhaps not, given her brother's unfair conviction and the absence of the mother whose motivations she was only beginning to comprehend.

Something in Shane became more intense, then settled, as if imparting greater understanding along with surprising peace. He didn't know if any of them would survive for much longer, but as for him, he accepted whatever was to come.

He wasn't fatalistic. Nor was he afraid. Not anymore. He was simply ready.

* * *

The first police unit entered the yard of the abandoned farm with its sirens and light bar off. Nevertheless, Jamie noted its arrival. This was precisely what she'd been waiting for.

"All right. Do you both understand what you're going to do?"

Marsha nodded soberly but Kyle was eager. "I'm gonna ninja him like this. Hey-yah!" The little arms imitated martial arts moves.

"Not this time," Jamie warned gently. "You have to help Memaw run down the stairs. Remember?"

"Uh-huh." Looking at her, he asked, "Then I come get you?"

"No, honey. I'm going to be doing something else. You can't come back inside. You have to go to the policeman and wait for your daddy. It's very important."

Although he made a face, he did agree. "Oh, okay."

"Good. Now, go stand where the door will open to hide you and be ready."

Jamie waited until the others were in place, then wrapped the child's jacket around her arm and gave the cracked window a hard whack. It made noise but didn't break.

Disregarding her own well-being, she hit the window again. This time it not only shattered, pieces fell out onto the porch roof.

Footsteps were thudding in the hallway. Jamie swept her wrapped forearm along the frame and broke away the last jagged remnants, then leaned out the window and yelled, "Go, go, go!"

The bedroom door flew open. Judge Randall burst in, cursing and shouting. He made straight for her as she'd planned, grabbed a fistful of her clothing and tried to jerk her backward.

She did the best she could to hang on to the sill and frame. To delay him. To keep him from getting past her to check the empty porch roof outside the window. She'd carried out her part of the plan. Now it was up to Marsha and Kyle to sneak past him while he was distracted, get down the stairs and out the front door.

Wide-eyed, Jamie saw a blow coming and raised her hands defensively. That was enough to deflect the attack but not to keep her from being stunned.

She fell backward.

Saw Randall start to lean out the window.

Heard him bellow as her head hit the floor.

The first thing Shane saw when he and Harlan arrived was a line of patrol cars parked on each side of his truck, providing a barrier against whoever was in the house. He was out of the sheriff's unit and racing toward a group of other officers long before the dust settled.

When the door of the farthest car opened and his son jumped out, he fell to his knees with open arms.

"I was a ninja," the boy told him happily as he threw himself at his daddy. "I saved Memaw. All by myself."

"That's wonderful," Shane managed to say while blinking back tears of relief.

The nearest uniformed officer said, "You folks need to keep your heads down and stay where you're told, for your own safety." He gestured. "We have Mrs. Bryce in that car. If you and the boy will join her…"

Rising as far as a crouch, Shane took Kyle's hand and led him. As promised, his mother was seated in the rear of the police car. There was an ice pack on her ankle.

"Are you all right?"

She clasped his hand. "I'm fine. Just twisted it running down the stairs."

As her eyes met his, Shane realized what she was not saying. Only she and Kyle had escaped.

"What about…"

"She got us out," Marsha told him. Sniffling, she wiped her damp cheeks. "She was amazing."

"The judge let you go?"

Marsha was shaking her head. "No, no. He's a raving lunatic. Jamie set up a trick, lured him away, and we were able to make it out."

"But…?"

"She's still in there, as far as I know." The older woman pulled her grandson onto her lap and held him close. "I was afraid none of us would survive."

Shane wanted to rejoice, and, in his heart, he did. Up to a point. There was only one thing wrong with Jamie Lynn's plan. It had not included saving herself.

The sheriff was conferring with the other officers when Shane returned to him. They were actually talking about standing back and waiting for the hostage negotiation team to arrive. That could take hours. And if the judge was as deranged as everyone believed, that was far too long.

"We need to at least try to talk to him," Shane insisted.

A murmur of voices vehemently disagreed. "Let the experts handle this," Harlan said above the din.

"We brought the boxes of Dad's papers he wanted."

"And he has the upper hand," the sheriff countered.

"According to your mother, he's not only armed and acting real crazy, he has one more hostage."

"I know. That's why I want to negotiate."

"Out of the question."

With that, the sheriff turned away as if dismissing Shane's concerns. It wasn't good enough. Sam would have done something, somehow. He had always managed to talk his way out of a jam. Except that last time, Shane reminded himself. The man who was holding Jamie at gunpoint was probably the same one who had arranged his dad's murder. That put him in a whole other category.

Shane tapped Harlan on the shoulder. "You need to bring Bobbi-Sue out here to talk to him."

"Why her?"

"Because she was involved at the beginning of all this. That's what Max had started to explain when he was shot. The hit-and-run driver had to be either her or Alan Abernathy. Their fathers conspired to blame Ray and got Max involved. He was trying to protect Martin."

"Ray Jr. confessed."

"That doesn't make him guilty. He was weak, worn down by the trial. Once he figured out what was happening he changed his plea for the sake of his family. Only it was too late to save his father."

"Alice was right?"

"Looks that way to me." Shane gestured toward the house. "Last I heard, Abernathy's son went to Texas, but Bobbi-Sue is still around."

"She teaches school, for crying out loud. She can't be guilty of murder."

"What she is or isn't guilty of doesn't matter now. All we need her for is to talk down the judge."

Reluctantly, the sheriff conceded. "All right. I'll radio for a deputy to fetch her. But there's no way I'm putting one of Serenity's model citizens in danger. She can sit out here in my car and use the bullhorn."

"Fine. Whatever." *Just do something*, Shane added silently, remembering how he'd accused Jamie Lynn of being impatient and wondering how he was going to force himself to wait for anything.

He eyed the cardboard boxes in the backseat of the sheriff's car. If he got them out and stacked them atop the car's trunk, Randall would be able to see them from the house and would know they'd complied with his demands. That wasn't guaranteed to help but it couldn't hurt.

The last box was in place when a shot was fired from an upstairs window.

It cut a round hole into a box mere inches from Shane's shoulder.

By the time he realized what had happened, he could easily have been felled by a second shot—just like Max.

The first thing that crossed his mind as he dived behind the car was, "Thank you, Jesus!"

"If you shoot at them, they're going to shoot back," Jamie warned her captor. "Are you sure that's what you want?"

He guffawed. "I'm an important man. They won't shoot me."

"Okay, if you say so. Still, I wouldn't stand in front of any windows if I were you."

"Think you're so smart, don't you? Well, you're not as smart as I am. You never guessed I was behind all your troubles, did you?"

She chose to humor him. "No, sir. I sure didn't. We were blaming Benjamin Abernathy."

"Oh, he was part of it. But he wanted to scare you away. I told him and told him, that girl won't scare any more than her stubborn daddy did."

"You killed my father?"

Another harsh laugh. "Not me. It wasn't hard to find somebody willing to do it. Throw enough money at any problem and you can make it go away."

"And my mother?"

The judge shook his head, his eyes hidden behind the night vision goggles. "Missed her. She ran off before I expected her to. It didn't seem wise to go after her. Now I wish I'd gotten rid of all of you."

"The way you got rid of Max Williford tonight?"

"Max is dead? Well, well. Looks like my old partner came through for me. I told Ben we needed to tie up all the loose ends. I guess he did."

"It was just you and Abernathy and Williford? I'm impressed. The three of you pulled off a slick frame."

"It was, wasn't it?" The judge sounded less manic and more resolved.

"The only thing I don't know," Jamie Lynn said, fighting to keep her tone soft, her voice even, "is which teenager was driving my brother's car that night."

"What difference does it make?"

"None, I guess. I'm just curious. If it wasn't your daughter, why did you take a chance on getting involved?"

Randall cursed under his breath and paced away from her. "Because the kids would never admit who was behind the wheel. They thought they were being clever. Getting their parents to bail them out no matter what. And it worked. I know Bobbi-Sue was in the car. She hit her mouth on the dash and loosened a couple of teeth."

The blood on the car seat! Jamie's heart thudded. Even if she didn't make it out of this alive so she could repeat what she'd learned, DNA should lead law enforcement to the guilty parties. Both of them. If Shane couldn't interest the famous Innocence Project in taking the case, he could still prevail upon the sheriff to have the samples tested.

But would he? Or would he be so glad to see the last of her he dropped the whole thing? Clearly, Judge Randall was going to jail and therefore Abernathy's actions would also come into question, but would that be enough to reopen R.J.'s case if there was nobody insisting on it?

Tears pooled behind her lashes as she considered her probable fate and rejected it. She was not ready to give up. Nor was she willing to let a madman win this battle, let alone the war. A person didn't have to be connected to law enforcement to crave justice. She might not be armed the way the judge was but she was far more cognizant of reality. He had the gun. She had the brains. Never mind that people in Serenity were probably seeing her as just as unbalanced because of her actions. What she had done to arrive at this point had been for the right reasons and she'd do it again in a heartbeat.

Kyle and Marsha were safe. Now it was her turn to escape.

How was yet to be determined.

EIGHTEEN

Shane had stayed down after the single bullet whistled past his ear. He eyed the house while armed men took defensive positions. If they went in, guns blazing, Jamie Lynn was likely to be collateral damage, providing the judge didn't start by shooting her. Given his demonstration of willingness to fire, anything was possible.

The pistol Shane carried was intended for defense, not offense. If he drew it and used it he was liable to be arrested. However, if he failed to act he could lose the one woman who had brought unimaginable blessings and new hope to his life.

Even before he drew the gun and checked it for readiness, his mind was on the move. There had been no more shooting. Spotlights from the police cars were trained on various openings, including the front-facing windows and doorway. That left the burned-out rear of the house essentially unguarded. He'd have to rely upon reflected light and the moon when it peeked out from behind wind-driven clouds, but that would suffice. It had to.

Shane skirted the east end of the line of parked cars, purposely avoiding alerting his mother and son. He was not planning to waste his life or leave Kyle fatherless. He simply intended to do whatever was necessary to save Jamie. Again. Whether the sheriff acknowledged it or not, Shane knew that was his God-given obligation.

Voices drifted to him before he cleared the detritus that had once made up the back porch and kitchen. Freezing to listen, he heard Jamie first. His heart twisted.

"You should involve the prosecutor in this, you know. He's as guilty as you are."

Randall shouted, "Who says I'm guilty? Do you know who I am? How important I am? Nobody will ever believe your lies about me."

"Sorry." The rest of her reply was too muted to make out but its tone indicated she was trying to placate the irrational man.

Gun pointing ahead, Shane took a few more steps. The broken, charred boards beneath his boots shifted. Cracked. Brought an exclamation from upstairs.

That was proof of where Randall was holding Jamie Lynn. It was also a good indication that the judge now knew he wasn't the only one in the house besides his prisoner.

"Who's there?" he called down.

Shane didn't move a muscle. As long as his adversary didn't know where he was, he still had a slight advantage.

"You'd better speak up or I'll shoot the woman!"

While Shane strained to see better in the dimness, a large form appeared on the topmost landing. It was too massive for one person. Clearly, the judge was using his captive as a human shield.

"I'm here," Shane answered. "I brought you my father's papers and old files."

"What for?"

That query was such a shock, Shane didn't know how to reply. "You—you asked for them."

"Why would I do that?"

Shifting his location each time he spoke, Shane hoped to keep the madman guessing. "You said you'd trade them for my family."

Laughing hoarsely, Randall stepped forward enough to catch a reflection from a spotlight on the chromed action of his rifle. Judging by its position, Shane surmised that the barrel was pointing at Jamie's head. "This one isn't family, yours or anybody's. She's a renegade. A nuisance. Nobody cares what happens to her, not even her stupid brother."

"I care," Shane said. He knew he was taking a chance by giving the judge more emotional leverage but he chose to do it rather than have Jamie think she didn't matter. They both needed all the hope, all the inner strength they could find, including that of their faith. "So does God," he added.

From the stairway came Jamie's loud "Amen!"

That outburst caused the judge to shift slightly. To adjust his hold.

Shane saw her legs lift as if she were about to kick a field goal with both feet.

Randall staggered.

Jamie's soles connected with part of the weakened banister and knocked it loose.

That threw her captor off balance. He teetered. Made a grab for the cracked railing and ended up grasping thin air.

With a shriek, Jamie Lynn lunged for the solid floor. Shane could hear her scrambling to stay up there. If he hadn't been too far away he'd have tried to catch her as she fell.

Instead, it was the judge who sailed off the second-floor landing. The rifle fired wildly, sending a bullet into the ceiling and making it rain plaster, before he crashed onto a pile of broken, charred wood and lay there, crumpled and unmoving.

"Jamie! Hang on, honey. I'm coming," Shane shouted, taking the stairs two at a time and holstering his own firearm.

His hands closed around her wrists. Held tight. "Gotcha."

Portable spotlights illuminated the scene as the police stormed in. Jamie Lynn's legs and feet were kicking like those of a floundering swimmer.

Shane eased her back onto the landing. "Are you hurt?"

"No. Just really, *really* scared."

He helped her stand, pulled her into his arms and cautiously peered down at the judge. "Is he dead?"

"Appears so," Harlan said. "How's the girl?"

Shane's hold tightened as he wrapped her in an embrace he had feared might never be possible again. "She's wonderful," he said. "Absolutely wonderful."

When Jamie raised her face to his, he proved his seriousness by kissing her. Soundly.

She was seated at the rear of an ambulance, wrapped in a scratchy gray blanket, when a stretcher left the old house bearing a body bag. So, Randall was really gone. It was hard to feel sorry for him, given his actions, yet she did. And for his daughter. The dire consequences of some sins never went away, did they?

A gloved EMT had been extracting wood slivers from her knees and palms. "That's all I can do out here," the young man said. "You'll need to see a doctor for the rest. Can I get you something to calm your nerves?"

"It's a tad late for that," she said with a slight smile.

She didn't want coddling, she wanted Shane. Desperately. They had been separated to be individually interviewed as soon as they'd left the old house. She hadn't seen him since. Given the horrendous evening they'd both had, she needed him near.

That thought broadened her smile. *Very, very near*, as in inseparable. The kind of closeness that she had never shared with anyone before. The kind reserved for one special person. The kind that lasted a lifetime.

Of course, there was no guarantee Shane loved her enough to set aside the prejudice created by his father's death, or to take a second chance on marriage, but she could hope. And pray. Just because the elements that had brought them together were not the usual boy-meets-girl events, that didn't mean their relationship was doomed.

Speaking of praying, she thought, closing her eyes and turning her thoughts heavenward. There had been plenty of opportunities to call out to God recently and she found that the more she prayed, the easier it got. The Lord had not changed, of course. She had.

As cars came and went she withdrew into herself, content to talk to God and quietly listen. It wasn't as if she heard celestial voices; it was more an overall peace and sense of comfort that had descended to blanket her.

A soft word spoken close by brought her back to reality. "How are you?" Logan Malloy asked.

Jamie Lynn was almost as glad to see him as she would have been if Shane had returned. "I'm okay. Judge Randall is dead. So is poor Max. He was trying to tell us about his son and the other kids when he was shot."

"I heard. I'm sorry. If I'd thought there was any danger I wouldn't have intervened."

"If I had known others might die I would have gone about this differently, too," Jamie told him. "I'd still have tried to clear my brother, though."

"Perfectly understandable." He hesitated and she glimpsed pathos in his gaze. "Is Shane around?"

"Yes. The sheriff took him away to get an official statement. Randall apparently lost his mind at the end. He was totally irrational."

"Everybody else is okay? You? Marsha? Kyle?"

Jamie nodded. "We're fine. We may have trouble convincing Kyle that he's not a superhero, though. In order to get him to cooperate and not pout, I told him it was his job to rescue his grandmother. He did such a good job he may want to make it a regular practice."

"All in good time," Logan said. "He can tell his class about it on Sunday and I'll have the teacher read the Bible story of David and Goliath."

"Just so Kyle doesn't have a sling for throwing rocks," she teased. "We don't want him demonstrating."

The pastor chuckled. "An excellent point. We could use somebody like you to help teach our kids. You understand the way they think." Pausing, he grinned at her. "Any chance you may change your mind and decide to stay on in Serenity?"

Gazing over his shoulder to where the officers had taken Shane, she shrugged. "I don't know yet. A lot will depend on how long it takes to get my brother a new trial."

"And on what Shane Colton thinks of your relocation?"

"I didn't say that."

Logan's grin widened. "You didn't have to. This is a great place to live and raise a family—most of the time. Don't let past disappointments influence your current choices. We'd love to have you stay."

Warmth crept up Jamie's neck to color her cheeks more. "Tell you what, Pastor. If Shane happens to ask, feel free to tell him how much I care about him and his son."

"Oh, no. That's going to be up to you."

"What if he rejects me?"

The older man patted the back of her hand, and she noticed a twinkle in his eyes. "You just faced down a raving maniac, rescued a child and his grandmother, then bested the same crazy man while he pointed a loaded gun at you. I think you can handle telling a nice guy like Shane that you've fallen in love with him."

Casting an insightful glance at the clergyman, Jamie arched her eyebrows and smiled. "From your lips to God's ears."

After his debriefing, Shane had headed back to rejoin Jamie Lynn, only to discover that she and the rest of his family had been taken to the local hospital. He couldn't get there fast enough.

Without stopping to ask where his loved ones were, he burst in through the ambulance entrance, not slowing until he'd reached the treatment cubicles. From there it was easy to follow the sound of his son's shrill voice.

"And then I hit him like this," the child said.

Shane was almost the recipient of a make-believe karate chop to the knee as he pushed back the weighted curtain.

There they were. All of them. Even Otis. Shane broke into a wide grin and hoped he wasn't actually going to shed a few tears of relief and joy.

"Oh, good, now we can start the celebration," Jamie Lynn said. "Where's the cake?"

Shane patted his son on the head, kissed his mother's cheek and shook hands with Otis as he worked his way toward his ultimate goal.

The bright sparkle in Jamie's eyes answered some of his questions but not all. He paused a few feet in front of her and waited as she stood. Nobody moved. Nobody spoke.

Finally, Shane asked, "Are you all right?"

"I am now." She averted her gaze, her cheeks warming.

"I meant what I said," Shane told her.

"When?"

He could tell that everyone in the exam cubicle was waiting for his reply, and although he did wish he could speak to Jamie Lynn privately, he wasn't willing to wait. Not after the night they'd all had.

"When I told the judge that you were part of my family, that I cared about you."

After taking a small step forward, she paused. "I suppose it's because I'm in shock, but I don't recall many details about tonight. Feel free to refresh my memory."

"I'll do better than that," Shane promised, opening his arms to her.

When she stepped into his waiting embrace, and he pulled her closer, she slid her arms around his waist and laid her cheek on his chest. "Mmm. Good start, Mr. Colton."

"Thank you, Miz Jamie Lynn. I aim to please."

In the background, Shane heard Otis snort, Marsha giggle and Kyle groan.

Jamie laughed softly. "That's quite a chorus we have serenading us. Too bad Otis left Useless in the car. He loves to sing along."

"This bunch sure needs to work on their harmony." Shane was so content, so elated, to have her in his arms and know that all his loved ones were safe and sound he could barely keep from shouting. As it was, his grin was so wide it was cramping.

Long, precious moments passed before he loosened his hold and eased her away so they were face-to-face. "I've been fighting my feelings," he said. "Tonight, when I thought I'd lost you, I had to admit them to myself. I care about you, about what happens to you, and I'd like you to consider staying in Serenity, maybe for the rest of your life."

"Only on one condition," Jamie replied softly.

Shane frowned. "Anything."

Her burgeoning smile and the twinkle in her misty eyes relieved most of his worry. "You have to promise that you'll court me like a true Southern gentleman and sweep me off my feet."

"I thought I already did that." Laughing, he waited for the humorous reply he knew was coming.

"Catching me when I'm about to fall off a stairway and break my neck doesn't count."

"Picky, picky, picky," Shane said just before he stepped back, took her hand and bowed at the waist. "All right. Miz Henderson, will you do me the honor of allowing me to escort you to the Serenity Homecoming celebration and terrapin races next week on the town square?"

"I thought you'd never ask." She curtsied. "I'd be delighted."

"Good. Since you're in the mood to accept invitations, how would you like to marry me, too?"

She sobered. "You're sure?"

"Yes. But I won't rush you. We can take as much time as you need."

"I'd like to put all the negatives behind me first. And I want to try to find my mother so she and Aunt Tessie can both come to our wedding."

"I already have Pastor Malloy working on it," Shane told her. "And the sheriff is going to reopen my dad's case, so your brother should be free soon, too."

"My hero." Jamie's lips trembled and her eyes filled with unshed tears.

Shane followed the urgings of his heart, tilted her chin up with one finger, bent and kissed her.

In the background he heard his son again. This time, the response was much better, probably due to Marsha's hushed explanations.

Kyle went "Ahhhh!" followed by, "Whoopee! I'm gonna get a mama!"

EPILOGUE

Jamie had been delighted to learn that the capture of Benjamin Abernathy had also resulted in the apprehension of his son, Alan. The prosecutor had insisted he had never suggested that anyone actually do away with Sam Colton. Alan had apparently overheard his father complaining about the sheriff and his teenage mind had misinterpreted that as a request for a violent solution.

Bobbi-Jo Randall had been given probation and had left town with her family to start a new life somewhere else. Alice Henderson had been located in Florida, using an alias, and had eventually been convinced she could come home without jeopardizing her daughter's welfare.

Jamie had barely recognized her mother after so many years and so much trauma, but joint trips to the beauty shop on the square had removed the gray from Alice's dark hair and helped restore her dimmed beauty. So had being reunited with her beloved daughter and being able to arrange a proper funeral for Ray Sr. And having R.J.'s conviction thrown out, so he could be released.

By the time they entered Serenity Chapel that special morning, Alice was glowing. She embraced Jamie

Lynn. "I'm so proud of you, honey. You're such a beautiful bride."

Jamie's eyes filled. "Hey, you'll make my mascara run."

"Shane will never notice."

"Maybe not, but Kyle will. He told me once that I looked like a raccoon!"

Alice laughed softly. "Children can be too honest sometimes."

"Little ones can." She thought of her brother. "It's when they get older that the trouble starts."

"And ends, thanks to you." Alice blotted her own tears with a lace-edged hanky. "I don't know how any of us can ever repay you."

"It wasn't just me, it was Shane and Pastor Malloy and Harlan and lots of others. I just gave them a little nudge."

"Little? When I think of how close you came to…"

Jamie touched her mother's thin arm through the voile of her long-sleeved dress. "Hush. That's in the past. It's time for a new start." She glanced out the choir room door where they'd been waiting and caught a glimpse of one of the regular Sunday ushers. "Maybe God has something special in store for you, too. Look who's hovering in the hallway."

"I've made lots of lovely friends since I started coming to church with you."

"Uh-huh. Keep talking."

"Oh, hush. Come on. You don't want to be late for your own wedding, do you?"

In truth, Jamie Lynn was on the verge of weeping for joy and was eager for distraction. She found it when she followed Alice out the door and spotted her future mother-in-law. Marsha had chosen a gown in a shade of mauve that complemented the mother-of-the-bride dress. In her arms was a formerly white dog with part of his hair dyed to match!

Jamie grinned and almost laughed aloud. "Oh, poor Useless. How could you?"

"I didn't. Your son did," Marsha explained. "I bought a bottle of dye to color my satin shoes and a certain little boy decided it would be fun to paint it on the dog, too. The groomer says he's sorry but it's permanent. It'll have to grow out."

"Well, his hair does go with my flowers." Reaching out, she ruffled her pet's ears. "Tell you what. Hand him to me and I'll carry both down the aisle."

Alice gasped. Marsha giggled. And Useless wiggled all over when Jamie reached for him.

"Okay, it's your party," Marsha said. "I'll be right up front and take him from you when you hand your bouquet to your bridesmaid."

And so it went. Jamie proceeded to the sanctuary and prepared to enter. Logan Malloy stood front and center with Shane and his attendant, her recently released brother. If it hadn't been for his tattoos, R.J. would have looked exactly like their late dad.

Jamie paused, waiting for Shane to see her and react to the recent addition to her bridal ensemble.

She knew the moment he understood what she was about to do because a broad grin split his face and amusement lit his countenance.

Halfway down the aisle, Useless caught the spirit of excitement and began to bark. Jamie heard their guests start to titter, then break into laughter.

Shane took a step forward and met her just short of

her destination. She wanted to giggle, to weep, to express astonishment that such a wonderful man wanted to marry her.

Leaning closer, he whispered, "I should have known you'd surprise me, but I never dreamed it would be this funny."

"I hope I keep you on your toes for the rest of your life," Jamie told him. She handed her little dog off to Marsha, then took the hand of her husband-to-be. It was warm. Comforting. Sure and steady. They were together with family and surrounded by old and new friends.

She was truly home.

* * * * *

Dear Reader,

I don't know what it would be like to experience the kind of life upheaval and injustice that Jamie Lynn Henderson has, but I have gone through others. We all have. And I don't know how I'd have managed without my faith in God and the assurance that He cares for me. No one else has the divine insight necessary to look ahead and see what the future holds; to guide us through. The only way I can continue to take a step forward, to face each new day, is by putting my trust in my Heavenly Father and His Son—in the best and the worst of times.

If you don't have the assurance that you're God's child, I urge you to seek it. All you have to do is surrender your pride, ask Jesus to forgive and accept you right now, and He will. It's that easy.

I love to hear from readers, by email VAL@ValerieHansen.com or at P.O. Box 13, Glencoe, AR, 72539. I'll do my best to answer as soon as I can, and www.ValerieHansen.com will take you to my website.

Blessings,
Valerie

COMING NEXT MONTH FROM
Love Inspired® Suspense

Available February 2, 2016

RANSOM • *Northern Border Patrol*
by Terri Reed
When Liz Cantrell's sister is kidnapped and a necklace is demanded as ransom, the antiques dealer must work with agent Blake Fallon to bring down a jewel smuggling ring—and keep her sister alive.

PLAIN DANGER • *Military Investigations*
by Debby Giusti
Speechwriter Carrie York never expected inheriting her father's estate near Amish country would put her in peril. But someone is targeting her, and now she must depend on Tyler Zimmerman—her military policeman neighbor—to survive.

NAVY SEAL SECURITY • *Men of Valor*
by Liz Johnson
Wounded navy SEAL Luke Dunham's top priority is returning to active duty—until he meets physical therapist Mandy Berg. A ruthless stalker is after Mandy, and Luke will risk anything to save her...even his career.

ROCKY MOUNTAIN PURSUIT • by Mary Alford
Presumed dead, agent Jase Bradford thought he'd left the CIA behind. But when Reyna Peterson, his former colleague's widow, shows up at his mountain hideaway with dangerous men on her tail, he can't turn away a woman in trouble.

INTERRUPTED LULLABY • by Dana R. Lynn
Police lieutenant Dan Willis finally tracks down Maggie Slade, who disappeared after her husband's murder months ago, and discovers he isn't the only one who's been searching for the new mother. The killer has found her, as well.

UNDER DURESS • by Meghan Carver
After thugs fail to capture attorney Samantha Callahan and her adopted daughter, her former law school classmate Reid Palmer offers his protection...and his help determining why the criminals are in hot pursuit.

REQUEST YOUR FREE BOOKS!

2 FREE RIVETING INSPIRATIONAL NOVELS
PLUS 2 FREE MYSTERY GIFTS

Love Inspired®
SUSPENSE
RIVETING INSPIRATIONAL ROMANCE

YES! Please send me 2 FREE Love Inspired® Suspense novels and my 2 FREE mystery gifts (gifts are worth about $10). After receiving them, if I don't wish to receive any more books, I can return the shipping statement marked "cancel." If I don't cancel, I will receive 4 brand-new novels every month and be billed just $4.99 per book in the U.S. or $5.49 per book in Canada. That's a savings of at least 17% off the cover price. It's quite a bargain! Shipping and handling is just 50¢ per book in the U.S. and 75¢ per book in Canada.* I understand that accepting the 2 free books and gifts places me under no obligation to buy anything. I can always return a shipment and cancel at any time. Even if I never buy another book, the two free books and gifts are mine to keep forever.

123/323 IDN GH5Z

Name _____ (PLEASE PRINT) _____

Address _____ Apt. # _____

City _____ State/Prov. _____ Zip/Postal Code _____

Signature (if under 18, a parent or guardian must sign) _____

Mail to the **Reader Service:**
IN U.S.A.: P.O. Box 1867, Buffalo, NY 14240-1867
IN CANADA: P.O. Box 609, Fort Erie, Ontario L2A 5X3

**Are you a current subscriber to Love Inspired® Suspense books
and want to receive the larger-print edition?
Call 1-800-873-8635 or visit www.ReaderService.com.**

* Terms and prices subject to change without notice. Prices do not include applicable taxes. Sales tax applicable in N.Y. Canadian residents will be charged applicable taxes. Offer not valid in Quebec. This offer is limited to one order per household. Not valid for current subscribers to Love Inspired Suspense books. All orders subject to credit approval. Credit or debit balances in a customer's account(s) may be offset by any other outstanding balance owed by or to the customer. Please allow 4 to 6 weeks for delivery. Offer available while quantities last.

Your Privacy—The Reader Service is committed to protecting your privacy. Our Privacy Policy is available online at www.ReaderService.com or upon request from the Reader Service.
We make a portion of our mailing list available to reputable third parties that offer products we believe may interest you. If you prefer that we not exchange your name with third parties, or if you wish to clarify or modify your communication preferences, please visit us at www.ReaderService.com/consumerchoice or write to us at Reader Service Preference Service, P.O. Box 9062, Buffalo, NY 14240-9062. Include your complete name and address.

SPECIAL EXCERPT FROM

Love Inspired
SUSPENSE

Inheriting her estranged father's house near
Amish country puts this speechwriter in grave danger.

Read on for a sneak preview of
PLAIN DANGER by **Debby Giusti**.

Bailey's plaintive howl snapped Carrie York awake with a start. The Irish setter had whined at the door earlier. After letting him out, she must have fallen back to sleep.

Raking her hand through her hair, Carrie rose from the bed and peered out the window into the night. Streams of moonlight cascaded over the field behind her father's house and draped the freestanding kitchen house, barn and chicken coop in shadows. In the distance, she spotted the dog, seemingly agitated as he sniffed at something hidden in the tall grass.

"Hush," she moaned as his wail continued. The neighbors on each side of her father's property—one Amish, the other a military guy from nearby Fort Rickman—wouldn't appreciate having their slumber disturbed by a rambunctious pup who was too inquisitive for his own good.

Still groggy with sleep, she pulled on her clothes, stumbled into the kitchen and flicked on the overhead light. Her coat hung on a hook in the anteroom. Slipping it on, she opened the back door and stepped into the cold night.

"Bailey, come here, boy."

Again the dog's cry cut through the night.